DANCE WITH HONEY

Dance with Honey

Determination and Forgiveness

A NOVEL

BY
C.M. HAROLD

PALMETTO
PUBLISHING

Charleston, SC
www.PalmettoPublishing.com

Dance with Honey©
Copyright © 2021 by C.M. Harold

Cover design by Barbara Aronica-Buck, bookdesigner.com
Cover image Adobe Stock by Coka

First Edition

Hardcover ISBN: 978-1-63837-802-0
Paperback ISBN: 978-1-63837-803-7
eBook ISBN: 978-1-63837-804-4

To the memory of my wonderful mother, grandmothers and aunts; I am who I am because of your unconditional love, your style and grace and nurturing support.

"When love comes to kiss you, don't hold back."
~ Rumi

"In all things, in all ways, and always, make love."
~ C.M. Harold

CONTENTS

Chapter 1

THE SOFT GOLDEN LIGHT COMING FROM the crystal chandelier above the table and polished brass sconces on the smoky-gray suede-covered walls cast a romantic glow in the private dining room.

And there was a faint aroma of food and wine, the men's cologne, her perfume, and the fragrance of calla lilies wafting through the air like a breeze. It was a captivating breeze, and it, along with the secrecy of the rendezvous and the electrifying chemistry she had with the men, made Helen feel everything was right and perfectly aligned for her to do what she was doing and allowing to be done.

Slow and long strokes, like licking a scoop of your favorite ice cream on a hot summer day, that's how Irving licked Helen's nipple.

"Señorita?" he whispered. "Por favor."

With a patient grip, he held the metal clasp with his thumb and index finger as he alternated from licking and sucking the tender, berried flesh in his mouth.

Helen knew he was pleading.

She could hear it in his tone. He was begging for permission to lower the zipper on her black jumpsuit. She had already given him permission to unfasten the bodice, which now pooled around her waist.

She glanced down at him as he suckled her breast. The gentle tugs from his mouth sent ripples of tiny shockwaves straight to her core. When he looked up with his gorgeous hazel eyes, she knew he was one of the finest men she'd ever laid eyes on. Dominican Republic blood from his grandparents ran through his veins, no doubt contributing to his exotic looks. From them, he had learned to speak Spanish fluently.

"*Mmm*," she moaned with wanton lust, and she knew she'd give him anything he wanted.

There was an easy, flowing rhythm building inside of her, a soft humming that was slowly, very slowly growing in intensity.

It had started the moment she'd walked into the private dining room and seen Brenner for the first time. He was the perfect gentleman, and she loved how he looked in his dark olive slacks and olive silk-blend shirt.

Under heavy lashes, she gazed at him. He was still sitting next to them, watching. His mocha-chocolate skin, perfect Nubian nose, obsidian eyes, and handsome face came together to give him a look that she thought was as sexy as sin.

When their eyes met, he gave her a luscious wink. Helen smiled and returned her attention to Irving, who was wearing a pair of black slacks and a black silk shirt with thin red stripes.

She lifted her hand from his shoulder and ran her fingers through his brownish hair, which, when it grew too long, would curl around your fingers.

Irving made a loud slurp as he suckled her harder, and a jolt of pure pleasure ripped through her body.

It was intoxicating, and she felt wild and promiscuous, sitting on the lap of a man who wasn't her husband while he licked her nipple like he owned it.

Irving popped the tender bud out of his mouth, but he still caressed her breast and the diamond lariat necklace that lay between her cleavage with feather-light touches. Never wanting to forget the rose-petal softness of her skin, Irving had already branded the feel of her in his mind.

"Señorita, can I lower this?" His words came out in a near whisper as he gently tugged on the clasp.

Looking into his eyes, she smiled.

She knew he probably had no idea how incredibly sexy he looked right now, with his wet, slightly kiss-swollen lips and a look of raw need beaming across his face.

"Yes, you may," she whispered a mere inch from his lips before giving him a light kiss.

"You are irresistible." She brushed her finger across his bottom lip and couldn't help breathing in the spicy scent of his cologne. It reminded her of ginger, cardamom, and patchouli.

"So are you," Irving said, not taking his eyes from hers as he started to ease the clasp down inch by inch.

Helen's pulse quickened as his fingers ran along the waistband of her silk panties. He was skillfully leaving behind a trail of heated caresses.

Brenner watched the two of them. His pulse rose and fell at the lascivious display before his eyes, and he felt so aroused that he didn't know how much longer he could wait. He took a sip of the dry white wine as he looked his fill. "Sweet," he said, remembering the taste of her nipples.

Irving cupped her bottom and nudged her from his lap and onto the padded leather seat, which was really a bench nearly as long and wide as a twin-size mattress.

"You're as light as a feather," he told her as he slid from underneath her. "Lie back for me," he added in a buttery tone as he stood.

His eyes never strayed from her. The nuances in her every movement were mesmerizing. No matter how slight or minute, his brain recorded everything.

As Helen reclined on the seat, Brenner stood and reached for her feet. He laid them where he'd been sitting.

She was now in a supine position, with only a leather throw pillow under her head.

Both men paused a moment, drinking in the sight of her. "You are a beautiful woman, Helen," Brenner said while Irving's eyes shimmered with desire.

"Thank you," she said, feeling a seductive power that she'd believed had been lost. She realized that wasn't the case when she saw the look in their eyes.

"Let me push this out of the way," Brenner said, sliding the table forward at least five feet, giving them plenty of room to move around.

As the table shifted, the ice cubes in the chiller clanked, and an empty wine glass wobbled.

The black calla lilies caught Brenner's eye, as did the silver platters with hors d'oeuvres, half-eaten, which had gone cold. It would be hours before they got around to eating.

He turned around, and that's when his breath caught in his throat.

Helen's arms were draped lazily above her head as she held the pillow beneath, and Irving was lowering the jumpsuit down from around her waist.

She glanced at Brenner, who stood there as if rooted in place, and watched his eyes roam freely and unhurriedly over her body as he swallowed multiple times and breathed deep, slow breaths.

She looked at Irving and saw a myriad of sultry emotions cascading down his face, and she smiled, realizing that she was the cause of every emotion.

The tops of her panties were visible, and little by little, her glistening, caramel-colored skin was exposed.

Irving looked at her, and when he did, she blew him a kiss.

Chapter 2

"YOU KNOW, WHEN I ASKED REE WHY our reservations were until closing, she said, 'You don't know what time pleasure will take you to,'" Brenner said as he glanced at Helen.

She was lazily drawing circles around her nipple while gazing at him.

He stood near the table and couldn't help but smile. It was early.

With passion-filled eyes, she turned her attention back to Irving, who was on the side of the bench by her knees.

"Which means we've got lots of time to have a whole lot of pleasure," Irving said as he continued lowering the jumpsuit down like a slow striptease.

He had never undressed a woman before, and she knew this experience had to feel both stimulating and foreign to him.

They were looking at her with such need, so palpable that you could see it swirling around them like a hazy fog.

She propped her head on her right arm.

The tiny change in position caused her breasts to sway, and at the sight of it, Irving's Adam's apple worked up and down as he swallowed the lump that had suddenly formed in his throat.

A smile swept across her face as she read his thoughts. He was anxious and feeling greedy.

Her finger drifted to her other nipple, and she teased it like she had done its twin.

While the threesome gazed adoringly at each other, a thought whispered across her mind. *You get one life, but you've clothed a good bit of yours in kind pleasantries and proper comportment. You've had too many days filled with doubt and too many nights lost without lust. But you've awakened, haven't you? And it's time you dress your life in some fancier things, like wearing baubles around your neck. Accent your life with whimsy. Let sensuality drape from your shoulders like a jeweled shawl and invite in lots of vivid moments that will conjure the feeling of bliss.* She sighed, thinking that this sounded shamelessly reassuring.

Helen eased her eyes up and down her lovers' bodies as they watched her.

What I am doing is sinfully wrong, she said to herself. *And while Walt has many faults, he doesn't deserve my infidelity. The ills that have infected our marriage are not totally his. I bear just as much blame. Year after year, I was too accommodating, undemanding, congenial, and quiet. By trying to please him, I lost myself. And I know my demure ways dried up his interest in me. Especially in bed.*

"You're taunting us, aren't you, my dear?" Irving said as he watched her rub her hardened nipple.

Helen looked into his gorgeous hazel eyes, but she didn't respond right away. *I know this is wrong, but I'm not turning back. I'm letting go.*

And that's what she did. She let go and freed herself from anything and everything that could hold her back from giving herself this indulgent, luxurious, but needed moment.

She was determined to reignite the spark in her life, and spending the day with these men was only the beginning.

"Yes, I am. Is it working?" she said, giving him a sassy little wink.

Instead of easing the garment further down her legs, Irving paused and ran two fingers over her exposed stomach.

"Oh! It's working, alright!" He dipped his fingers into her navel and ran small circles around its whorl until he felt her muscles quiver.

She hadn't noticed that Brenner had eased closer until she felt him lift her ankle.

He removed one of her shoes and dropped it to the carpeted floor with a soft thud. He then freed the other shoe and caressed the bottom of her soles.

Looking down at her feet, he said, "Your toes are pretty!"

She smiled.

Brenner placed her feet on the bench and stepped aside while Irving moved to the foot of the bench and continued with his task. "I've got to get this off!" He chuckled.

Ahh! So, this is what double-teaming feels like. She laughed to herself.

"Helen, don't move. Let us do all the work." Irving lifted both of her bare feet and rested them on his hard thighs to make it easier for him to remove her clothing.

She looked at him. *All kinds of thoughts must be running through his head. I wonder if this will be a one-time thing for them, or will they spice up their sex life by bringing women into their bedroom?* Her hand stilled. *'Cause his fine ass is practically drooling.* She chuckled under her breath.

"Don't stop." Irving inclined his head towards her breasts.

"Yes, sir," she said playfully. She stuck her index finger in her mouth and wet it, and then she started caressing her nipple again.

"Yes, just like that." Irving winked at her. He tugged the legs of the jumpsuit over her ankles, pulling the garment free.

"Wow!" He took a deep breath at her sheer beauty as his lustful eyes raked over her body, covered only by her wispy black silk panties.

He'd seen women naked before, in *Playboy* magazines and porn movies, and his two sisters when they were little girls, but this was his first time standing in front of a virtually naked woman.

Brenner smiled. "Helen, it's been a lifetime since I've been with a woman. Even then, I didn't have a true desire for that. But I can tell you, from the moment I laid eyes on you to seeing you lying here, I will never, ever get enough of you. I will always want more of you." Brenner spoke softly, yet his voice had dropped an octave, making him sound sinful.

He ran a finger down the lariat necklace, which sparkled under the chandelier lighting. His finger brushed against her flesh, light as a gentle breeze. She shivered at his touch.

He leaned down. "You are amazing," he whispered against her lips before giving her a kiss.

She sighed softly when their lips touched. He was melting her on the inside, turning her into a liquid puddle of cream.

When the kiss ended, she turned away and looked into Irving's eyes. He was staring at her like she was a goddess. It made her feel confident, sexy, and so incredibly bold.

Brenner smiled at Irving. "This is what you wanted, isn't it?" He gave his partner a wink.

Irving returned the smile and looked at Helen. "You know, I'm not ashamed to admit that I've never seen a woman's body in real life. Dreams and pictures in magazines don't count, so the honor is all yours."

There was a shyness to his chuckle.

"And I must tell you. You simply take my breath away." His voice couldn't hide his growing affection.

She noticed his barely perceptible shake. "You're trembling."

"Babe, you got this," Brenner said in an encouraging tone. "I know this is probably an out-of-body moment for you. Just go with the flow."

"Not to worry, you two. I'm good!" Irving looked at the two of them and smiled. "Matter of fact, I'm great!"

She still caressed her nipple, but her eyes followed his as he came towards her.

"Let's see what's under this." There was a huskiness in his voice as he secured the edges of her panties with his thumbs and index fingers.

Before she knew what he was doing, he leaned down and gave her nipple a quick little suck. Her finger got sucked into his mouth as well.

"*Mmm*. Your hands aren't trembling now," she teased.

Irving met Brenner's eyes. "I told you. I've got this, Bren!" He winked at his partner and slowly traced a whimsical curlicue over her stomach.

"Alright!" Brenner laughed and then looked down at Helen.

"You okay, baby?" He had moved to the top end of the bench.

She glanced at him, meeting his obsidian eyes. *I could look into his eyes forever.* "Yes, baby. I'm perfect." Her tone evinced the growing intimacy between them.

Irving stopped and looked at her. "Didn't I tell you I was a jealous lover?" His eyes had darkened.

Her pulse quickened at the subtle yet playful reprimand in his tone. "You did," she whispered.

Irving pretended to be annoyed. "You callin' my man baby, and he's callin' you baby…" He paused, glancing from Helen to Brenner.

Brenner hunched his shoulders, feigning innocence.

"What about me?"

Helen chuckled. "Irving, baby, I'll make it up to you," she said softly. Cupping both of her breasts, she gave her nipples a hard pinch.

"Oh, my!" Brenner groaned low in his throat.

"Yes, that's better, but you're going to have to do more, much more, to make it up to me," Irving teased, knowing for the first time in his life that his body, particularly a certain part of his anatomy, was stirring with sensations brought on by a woman.

She smiled and, like a temptress, continued to lie there, letting them do all of the work.

Irving began lowering her panties.

She felt the smooth tug of the silk fabric as it eased down her body and watched as her patch of tiny brown curls appeared. *Soon I'll be totally naked*, she thought, feeling the wicked licks of lust streak a path straight to the tips of her pedicured toes.

Brenner reached for her hands, resting above her head. "Give me your hands," he whispered as he gently clasped them in his.

"Ahh, double-teaming me again," she said, meeting Brenner's eyes moments before she was stripped bare.

"My, oh, my!" Irving said as he tossed the weightless panties on the table. His eyes were a kaleidoscope of swirling brown shades.

"Damn! You're perfect in every way," Brenner said in a voice that didn't mask his impatience.

My, oh, my, indeed, she thought as her pulse began to race.

Irving could wait no longer; he had to taste her. Staring into her eyes, he willed her not to look away.

She watched as he got on the bench and crawled between her legs. Inch by slow inch, he neared the apex of her thighs.

She inhaled deeply; being seduced by these men had her senses reeling, as they were ravenous.

He laid his hand on her thigh and gently pushed her leg open wider until it draped over the side of the bench.

"Baaaby," she moaned. Butterflies fluttered in her stomach.

He could smell her scent. It was unlike anything he had smelled before, but it reminded him of the sweet scent of gardenias. He inhaled, filling his lungs with it.

"My señorita," he whispered. "Can I taste you?" He lowered his head to her core and nuzzled his nose in the patch of curls, breathing in.

His growing erection throbbed against his zipper. This moment was so far outside of his normal self that, absent his reflection in the mirrored wall, he wouldn't believe this was him. But it was, and he dug the hell out of it.

"Don't make me wait any longer, Irving." She gave him a naughty smile.

To say Helen was floating on a cloud would have been an understatement. She was the cloud.

He took another deep breath until satisfied that he'd infused her sweet smell deep within him. Then, like a starving man, he began licking her. Gentle and unsure at first, his licks soon became slow, long, and urgent.

He was tasting and swallowing her essence, which was as yummy as butterscotch candy.

"Yes, Irving, baby. Ooh, that feels so good." She breathed and squirmed under his lustful assault.

He growled low in his throat as he licked her more and more and more.

"*Mmm*," she moaned, feeling his wicked tongue.

"You like that?" Irving whispered, not breaking contact with the tiny morsel snug in his mouth.

"*Yessss*." She sighed, gazing at the top of his head as he opened her legs wider. Her pulse raced, and her stomach rose and fell with her panting breath as her mind began to splinter like shards of glass.

"*Mmm*," she breathed. Her grasp on reality was slipping by the minute feeling Irving's skillful tongue.

"Baby?" Brenner leaned over her and gently lifted her chin. She could smell his masculine cologne.

"Open your mouth," Brenner said softly.

She tilted her head back, and he eased his tongue inside. His decadent, chocolatey taste still lingered in her mouth.

As one man thoroughly licked her and the other kissed her with a consuming force, her stomach muscles clenched, and soon she let out a gut-wrenching moan, nearly coming off the bench as an orgasm ripped through her body.

Chapter 3

IRVING LOOKED AT HELEN. A SATISFIED, lustful smile was on his face as he slowly backed off the bench.

Brenner gestured with his finger. "Come here. Let me taste the two of you."

As Irving made his way over, Brenner couldn't stop himself from easing his eyes down his body.

"Hey, you!" Brenner whispered moments before Irving stepped into his embrace.

"Hi, babe."

"How are you feeling?" Brenner knew that they would have a lifetime of conversations about this woman and this day, but he was most curious about what was on Irving's mind at this moment.

"I'm super fantastic!" Irving grinned.

"Seeing you happy makes me happy!"

Brenner pulled Irving close, wrapped his arms around his waist, and kissed his mouth in a possessive way. Their tongues mated, and he could taste Helen's feminine essence. Combined with his partner's, the mix was incredibly exotic.

Perfect, he thought, ending the kiss. "Yes. Nice, very nice, indeed." He swallowed the taste in his mouth before rubbing his finger along Irving's glistening bottom lip.

Helen watched the men. The love and passion between them were real, and it was plain to see they belonged to each other, fully and wholly.

With Irving snug in his embrace, Brenner looked at her. "You okay, baby? You want to take a little break, perhaps?" There was a softness in his attentive tone.

With languid movements, she shook her head. "I'm fine," she said softly. She shifted her gaze to Irving, "I'm actually super fantastic!" A smile lit the corners of her eyes.

"I love hearing that!" Irving winked.

"Well alright! We've got two super fantastic people and all day to have fun." Brenner came to her side, moving with fluid ease for a tall, built man.

He leaned down and brushed a strand of her hair behind her ear.

"We need to make it three super fantastic people," she whispered, feeling the warmth of his body.

As he looked into her eyes, he kissed her tenderly while caressing her breasts and stomach with feather-light strokes. The memory of their first kiss was still fresh in his mind.

"I like the sound of that." He ended the kiss, and as he walked to the foot of the bench, he slowly traced a trail down to her toes.

Her flesh sizzled as if his finger was a lightning bolt.

He watched her, never taking his eyes from hers. "I can't wait to taste you for myself," he said as he unbuttoned his shirt, giving her his version of a striptease.

"Brenner," she whimpered, aching for his touch.

"I know, baby. I'm anxious, too." He pulled his shirttails free and undid the remaining buttons.

They were drawn to each other like bees to honey.

Her stomach rose and fell with every inpatient breath as she glimpsed his toned chest and abdomen.

He unbuckled his belt and released the clasp on his pants.

This hedonistic day, he'd never forget. When he saw the pure need on her face, he realized it would change him forever. He was burning with desire for a woman, and the realization of this, something that he thought impossible, unsettled him. He'd deal with this revelation later.

"Baby." Helen sighed with lust as he eased on the bench and crawled between her legs.

His obsidian eyes locked on hers, and he became a predator stalking his prey.

He savored the heated look in her eyes as their anticipation built. *I'm going to enjoy every moment of this,* he said to himself.

When he touched the inside of her lower legs, she trembled.

"Shhh. It's okay, baby," he said soothingly as he looked into her eyes.

Standing at the top end of the bench, Irving reached for her arms. "Give me your hands. I want to hold you hostage. Not let you get away."

Helen glanced up, and they shared a sensual smile. She raised her arms, and Irving held one hand in each of his.

A moment later, she lowered her eyes and looked at Brenner as he gently bent her legs.

He pushed them outward and towards her midsection. As he held her legs firmly in place, a growl, low in his throat, escaped at the sight of her womanhood. He knew that he was seconds away from giving them what they both lusted for.

Her scent reached out to him. It was the sweetest perfume he'd ever smelled. He breathed in deeply and thought of honeysuckles after an early-morning rain. He wanted her scent to lodge down deep within him, and as wrong as it was, he needed her scent to become a part of him.

Irving bent down and kissed her wrists.

Helen looked up at him, and they shared a tender kiss.

With a hunger in his eyes, Brenner licked his lips when their eyes met, and he tightened his hold on her legs, ready to taste her.

He lowered his mouth to her core and began eating her alive.

The instant his tongue touched her, she moaned in ecstasy.

"Yes," Brenner groaned. "You taste so good," he whispered.

"*Mmm*," she murmured as his tongue created a rhythm for her to wantonly ride.

"That's it. Give it all to me." His voice had a sultry undertone.

"Yes." She writhed greedily and without shame, trying to get closer to his wicked mouth.

Just as greedily, he licked, sucked, and lapped her everywhere, as if his job were to leave no area untouched or untasted.

"*Ooh*," she sighed as pleasure burst through her body like sparks and flames from a firecracker.

Her creamy essence flowed freely into his mouth, and he coated his tongue with her DNA and swallowed every drop.

One minute, he'd lick her, and the next, he'd lap up her essence as if dying from thirst.

She felt like his tongue was a branding iron, as a hot, searing heat penetrated right through her womanly core, scorching and caressing every atom and cell in her body.

"*Ahh*," she moaned, starved for this moment. All she could do was moan at his intoxicating lovemaking. Her mind and body were floating in space, as he'd left her buoyant and weightless.

Brenner kept her under his spell, and his tongue continued to work its magic. When he thought she couldn't take it anymore, he gave her much more and stuck his tongue deep within her, moving it around in slow circles.

Irving watched her; he loved seeing lust and passion dance across her face. He bent down and started kissing and licking around her mouth, unknowingly matching the same circular motions as Brenner's tongue that was still buried deep inside of her.

These men were driving her certifiably "straight-jacket" CRAZY.

The intensity and thoroughness of Brenner's licking and sucking shattered her into ten thousand tiny pieces, making her wild. With reckless abandon, she bucked against his mouth repeatedly, trying to get closer, trying to get more of his wicked tongue.

Irving released her mouth, and she helplessly thrashed her head from side to side like a woman out of control, and as the orgasm ripped through her, she screamed so loud that it reached the stars.

Brenner couldn't take his eyes from her as he watched the orgasm hum through her body like a lover's melody, a melody that he'd given her.

After a very long moment, her eyelids droopy and heavy from passion, she looked at Brenner and smiled, and he blew her a kiss.

"My love," he whispered.

Chapter 4

THROUGH HIDDEN SPEAKERS, LESLIE ODOM Jr. sang "Autumn Leaves." Many things about this day would stay with Irving forever. This song was now part of the collection of memories.

"I like this song." He eased his eyes over her face, resplendent with a delicate shimmer of perspiration on her forehead.

She listened to the lyrics. "It's nice! He's got such a smooth sound."

"I agree." Irving swayed to the music and snapped his fingers. "Would you like something to eat or drink, or do you want to take a break?"

"I need to excuse myself for a moment." She brought her feet to the side of the bench and allowed him to assist her up.

"Hi, baby. Perfect timing," Brenner said, bringing her a one-size-fits-all white bathrobe.

Each of the private dining rooms had its own guest bathroom, well stocked with luxurious travel-size toiletries, toothbrushes, mouthwash, and face and hand towels, along with two guest bathrobes.

"Thank you," she said, sliding it on and then tying the sash.

"*The fallen leaves drift by my window…*" Irving sang, and he reached for her hand. She took his, and they laughed and swayed to the music.

Moments later, he released her hand, and she twirled over to Brenner.

She smiled as he playfully wrapped his arms around her waist. "*Fallen leaves of red and gold…*" he sang close to her ear as the two of them swayed side to side.

Irving took a sip of wine, enjoying this light, fun moment. *You're the only woman I want to be inside of. The only one I want in my memories,* he thought, watching them dance.

When the song ended, she stepped out of Brenner's arms. "I'll be right back." She looked at the two men before making her way to the bathroom.

"Are you hungry?" Brenner asked. "Do you want to look at the menu? Maybe order something?"

She loved their attentiveness. What woman wouldn't?

Standing at the threshold, she glanced over her shoulder. "I am hungry." She winked. "But not for food," she said with a sexy tone before closing the door to the sound of laughter.

"That's music to my ears!" Irving said to Brenner.

Ten minutes was all it took for her to use the toilet, wash her hands, and blot her face and neck with a cold towel. She didn't bother brushing her teeth, as she rather liked the taste of their kisses in her mouth.

Looking in the mirror, she saw her reflection. Her lips were kiss-swollen, and her eyes cloudy with lust and love. Her hair was tousled from their fingers running through it. She liked that and left it messy and uncombed.

Still gazing in the mirror, she realized she was a different woman.

Her body was alive in sensual ways, and vibrations from her orgasms sizzled through her like live wires brought down by a storm.

"Just wow!" She shook her head in amazement, turned away from the mirror, and left the bathroom.

When she came out, Irving walked over to her. "Here, taste this." He fed her a cold appetizer. It was a fresh fig square topped with fig preserves and a thin-sliced heirloom tomato and sprinkled with crushed walnuts.

"Umm, delicious. These are just as great cold," she said, swallowing the culinary delight.

She slid out of the bathrobe and let it fall to the floor. Both men cleared their throats as they watched her curvy bottom and hips sway as she walked.

She lay down, shifted onto her side, and propped her head up with her right hand.

"So…" she said, suggestively gazing at Irving.

Brenner smiled and gave his partner a tender kiss. He put on his black cloak and left the room, giving them their privacy. On the way out, he told them that he would wait in the car, and he asked Irving to call him when it was time for him to return.

When the door closed and they were alone, Irving took a deep breath and made his way to the foot of the bench. "So…" he said, letting his voice trail off. He slipped out of his shoes.

"You say you're hungry."

"For you."

Chapter 5

IRVING'S AND HELEN'S EYES LOCKED TO-
gether, and the raw desire in hers relieved the bit of nervousness that
he felt.

I'm free. Free to be whoever I want to be in this moment, he said to
himself as he started unbuttoning his shirt and pulling it out of his
pants. When the last button was undone, he unfastened the cuffs and
then took his shirt off and dropped it on the floor.

"Very nice," she whispered, letting her eyes roam down his broad
chest to the indention of his navel and his trim waist. His sun-kissed,
light complexion was un-marred by tattoos or marks. *Talk about eye
candy*, she thought, taking in his muscly abs and buff arms.

"Do you like what you see?" he asked, releasing his belt buckle and
unzipping his pants.

"Yes. Very much." Without taking her eyes off of him, she watched
as he lowered his pants. She eased a finger in her mouth, enjoying his
striptease.

At the sight of his black cotton briefs hugging his toned legs, she
felt her pulse rising. She knew what came next.

She didn't have to wait long.

"Wow!" She whispered and bit the tip of her finger as she gazed at the size of him. Her smile widened. He was gloriously made and standing in front of her naked and ready.

"You are sheer male perfection."

"Thank you," he said softly. Unable to wait any longer, he placed his knee on the bench and inched his way forward. His eyes never left hers.

He couldn't deny the nervous energy racing in his veins, but from the beginning, he had been comfortable with her. He felt safe unfolding his truths.

As he settled on top of her, the feeling of her skin against his was something that he'd never forget. She felt like silk. "*Umm.* Your skin is buttery soft." He said, framing her face with his hands.

"Thank you, baby." She smiled and ran her fingertips up and down his toned arms in slow, caressing strokes.

She looked into his eyes, which had darkened to a toasted amber. "I love the way you feel on top of me," she said sweetly, getting comfortable with the weight of his body.

"Helen, I don't think you'll ever know how special I feel that you are the woman I will have this moment with. You are my queen," he said seconds before taking possession of her mouth and giving her a passionate kiss.

As their tongues mated, she wrapped her arms around his neck and held him close.

He was erect, hard as a blade of steel and perfectly positioned at her vaginal opening. He throbbed and ached, eager to get inside of her.

Moving his hands down to her waist, he took a deep breath and quieted the butterflies fluttering in his stomach. "You know, I've never done this before." He eased his way into her hot, wet core, and the moment he felt her warmth and tightness encase him with a soft, muscly grip, it stole his breath, and he growled low in his throat.

"*Mmm*, baby." She sighed. The feel of him inside of her was simply wonderful. "Do you like it?" She wondered what was going through his mind.

"Amazing!" he said in a guttural tone as he cautiously began to move in and out of her. Hearing the pleasure in her voice relaxed him. *I must be doing this right.* He smiled inwardly and started thrusting harder and with more finesse and confidence.

"Yes, you feel amazing." He licked her ear, leaving a sloppy, wet trail around the outer edges.

She sighed and ran her fingernails along his shoulder blades, lightly brushing his skin.

"*Ooh*, yes," he said as he thrust inside of her in an age-old dance. The feeling was so delicious that they both moaned loudly.

As he pounded, moving in and out with force, her emotional grid went haywire. She couldn't describe how she felt as her emotions started colliding and tripping over the other as so many emotions ran through her at once.

He stroked her a bit faster, and when he did, he eased a hand between their bodies and cupped her left breast. He kneaded it and teased her already hardened nipple.

He made a guttural noise as the need to bury himself deeper within her took over.

From the first moment he'd been between her legs, feasting at her core, he had let go of the dream he'd had that had served as his guide. With Helen, he let himself go, let himself feel his way through with her as his guide. She was the only tutor he needed, and she taught him well.

Thrusting back and forth, going deeper and deeper, he groaned, "*Ooh*... This feels so good." The feeling was indescribably indescribable.

"*Mmm*," she moaned.

"Yes," he said as her inner muscles clenched him tighter.

She closed her eyes as a perfect orgasmic storm brewed inside of her.

"Please open your eyes, baby. I want you to look at me. See what you're doing to me," he begged.

She opened her eyes. They were dreamy, but she looked directly at him and smiled. And when she did, he rewarded her by rubbing her clitoris with his thumb. Not letting up, he thrust faster and deeper.

She whimpered and squirmed beneath him. "Ir...Irving." She breathed his name as strong sensations burned through her like a wildfire.

Digging her nails in his shoulder blades, she moaned, "*Baabby.*"

As he watched her face, Irving loved how it contorted and twisted with sensual pleasure—pleasure that he was giving her.

"You like that?" Irving murmured. He was still caressing and stroking her clitoris, stoking the fire inside of her.

"*Mmm*," she moaned as a rush of sensations consumed her.

"Tell me. Do you like it?" he demanded.

"*Um. Yes, baby, yess!*" she screamed moments before an orgasm exploded through her.

Irving continued taking her higher, and when her inner muscles clenched him tightly, milking him, it sent him over the edge, and he growled as his body shuddered from an orgasm that ripped through him with the heat of lava, searing a path straight to his soul.

As his seed spilled inside of her, he felt like the luckiest person on earth because he had his dance with honey.

* * *

After Irving and Helen had cuddled in each other's arms for several long minutes, he called Brenner and told him to come back.

Brenner had been waiting patiently in the car, but now it was his turn. He intended to straddle her across his lap, but only after taking her hard against the suede-covered wall.

Helen, Brenner, and Irving didn't get around to ordering more wine or their entrees or desserts until many hours later.

Chapter 6

WHAT A DAY IT HAD BEEN.

The sun was just below the horizon, casting the sky into nautical dusk.

A jazz instrumental played over the hidden speakers, and the smell of sex hung in the air, heavy like it had been sprayed from a bottle. Flickering candles stood on the table, which was littered with dirty dishes and empty platters, and golden flecks of light from the chandelier bounced off the walls.

All three had dressed and donned their black cloaks.

Helen's white-feathered masquerade mask was in the gift bag, along with the Yswara candle that Irving had given her. Her small clutch was leaning against the bag. Both were on the floor by her feet.

Brenner and Irving had stuffed their masks into their pants pockets.

"I don't wa…want to…go," Helen said in a broken whisper as she looked at both men. Unshed tears pooled in her eyes.

"We don't want you to go, either, my love," Brenner said softly as he wrapped his arms around her waist, still needing to touch her. "But you've got a long drive home, and I don't want you on the road by yourself so late."

"Don't cry, my queen," Irving said, wiping away the single tear that rolled down her face. His tone was so sweet that it soothed her.

He, too, needed to touch her.

"When you pull into your driveway, I want you to call and let me know that you've made it okay." Brenner leaned down and kissed her forehead. "You remember my number?"

"Yes," she said softly, breathing in his scent. It was a potent, masculine mixture of love, lust, and spices. "*Umm*," she said with a sigh. "I love the way you smell." She looked up at him.

Brenner gazed down at her, and the look in his eyes was that of a man who had fallen in love.

Going against the Ree & Mosley Agency rules, they had exchanged phone numbers. Also, she knew where they lived and worked, and they knew where she worked. But the men didn't want to know her home address, and she agreed that this, perhaps, was best.

Helen took a deep breath.

She smiled a little. "I remember both of your numbers and where you work and live." She tapped her temple. "I've got it up here."

"Don't forget. After the call, I want you to delete the number. I don't want you to have any problems."

"Yes, sir, counselor. I will," she teased while studying Brenner's handsome face.

He seemed to be doing the same as he stood there, leisurely gazing at her. "You are beautiful, my love."

"My love" and "my queen" had become the men's terms of endearment for her. She'd always remember how wonderful it made her feel to hear these words.

When Helen eased her eyes over to Irving, he held out his arms. Like a treasured woman, she stepped from one embrace to another.

"Irving," she said, looking into his hazel eyes.

He wrapped his arms around her and pulled her close.

Helen molded her body against his, snuggling in the places that she'd opened up.

Irving leaned down and whispered in her ear, "Thank you, my queen. You are forever in my heart."

"Both of you are forever in mine." Standing on the tips of her toes, she planted a kiss on his lips.

"*Umm,*" Irving groaned softly as he framed her face with his hands. He rained kisses all over her hair, the sides of her face, her ears and neck. "I love you! I love you! I love you! I love you!"

Helen giggled, feeling delicious flutters in her stomach. She reached up and placed her hands on top of his, which still framed her face.

Never in her wildest imagination did she think today would turn out so utterly perfect.

"Enough of that! Come here, you!" Brenner chuckled and tugged on her cloak.

Playfully rolling his eyes and shaking his head, pretending to be annoyed, Irving released her.

She once again stepped into Brenner's warmth. "Hello, you!" she said as a huge smile bloomed across her face.

Brenner leaned down. "Kiss me," he whispered against her lips.

With one hand holding the back of her head, he slid the other around her waist before taking possession of her mouth with such force that her knees literally buckled.

He held her tight while feasting on her lavish taste.

When he ended the kiss, he brushed his middle finger across her bottom lip.

Gazing into her eyes, he smiled. "I love you, Helen."

If she were a magician, she would bottle up this day. Make a perfume that she could dab on the insides of her wrists and behind her ears. One whiff would take her back to this day.

Brenner loosened his hold, and she eased from his embrace.

Instantly she felt adrift, missing the touch of his body, which anchored her so well. She knew that if she didn't leave soon, in another second, she'd be on her knees, begging them to let her stay.

Helen teared up again as she looked at both men. Men she had fallen madly in love with.

She took a deep, settling breath. "Irving and Brenner..." She paused to wipe the corner of her eye. "I came here today because I needed to do something to reclaim myself. To reclaim passion in my life. And I thought I was just having lunch with one man." She chuckled softly. "Irving, when you joined us today, everything got so much sweeter, so much better. It was perfect." Her voice trailed off as tears began to roll down her face.

"Don't cry, baby," Brenner said, reaching out to wipe away her sadness. "You're going to make Irving cry, and you know how sensitive he is." He chuckled and glanced over at his partner.

"Oww," he said, grabbing his arm. "You didn't have to hit me." He laughed and lightly punched Irving's bicep.

Irving rolled his eyes, ignoring Brenner. "Baby, we're just trying to cheer you up. Is it working?" There was a hopeful lightness in his tone.

Helen smiled. Using the back of the cloak, she dried her eyes. "Yes, it is. I still don't want to go, but I feel a little better."

She swallowed the lump in her throat and took a deep, calming breath.

"I know you will think I'm crazy…" She paused and looked at them. Seeing only love gave her the courage to continue.

"But I have fallen madly in love with both of you," she said softly before standing on the tips of her toes.

She wrapped her arms around Irving's neck. "I love you, Irving," she said before sealing her love with a sweet kiss.

When their lips parted, he lightly patted her on the butt. "I love you, too, my queen." His smile was so luminous that it brightened his eyes to the color of a crisp autumn leaf.

She'd never forget his beautiful eyes.

As she stepped over to stand in front of Brenner, she felt monarch butterflies in her stomach, but it was the sultry way he looked at her that stirred her insides, turned everything to liquid silk.

Helen eased up on her tiptoes and wrapped her arms around his waist, and he did what came naturally. His hands palmed her backside as he pulled her in real close.

"Brenner," she whispered. His name now rolled from her lips with ease.

"Yes," he said, nibbling at the corners of her mouth.

"Baby," she moaned. "Oh, Brenner, I love you."

He slid his tongue in her mouth, giving her one last passionate kiss. Their tongues mated and danced until a soft moan escaped from both of them.

A long moment later, he released her.

Helen's pulse was racing, and on wobbly knees, she stepped away from his embrace. Her tears were flowing freely now, running down her face like a river.

She reached down for her mask. Even though her eyes were blurry and her fingers trembled, she hooked the elastic bands around her ears, concealing her face and identity.

She picked up her gift bag and clutch, and without another word, she lifted the hood over her head.

Before leaving, she scanned the luxurious private dining room, taking in its suede-covered walls, the chandelier, the table, the leather bench.

All that was left now was one last look at the two men standing in front of her. Their hands were in their pockets as they watched her as intently as ever.

Although she was leaving to go home, in the most intimate way, she wasn't leaving them. Not really. They'd always be inside of her, and knowing this settled her.

Helen looked into their waiting eyes, first Irving's and then Brenner's.

"Goodbye," she whispered.

The men blew her kisses, and when the kisses landed on her like cupid's arrows, Helen opened the door and walked out.

Chapter 7

SHE CAME OUTSIDE. AS SHE STOOD UN-
der the porte cochere, the warm evening breeze ruffled and lifted the
folds of her cloak.

"Good evening, miss," Frank said, opening the back passenger-side
door of the black Cadillac CTS.

She had called him to let him know she was ready.

He could barely see her face under the hood and feathered mask.

With a brief glance, Helen met his eyes. "Thank you," she said,
stepping into the car. Instantly the coolness of the interior whispered
across her face.

A sports channel was playing from the speakers. The raucous com-
mentators would have to stand in for any casual conversation on the
ride back.

Helen wasn't up to it, and somehow she suspected that Frank knew
not to expect it.

He helped her gather up the flowing fabric of the cloak.

"Thank you, Frank," she said as she settled in the backseat. She adjusted the garment, making it comfortable to sit on, and unfastened the front bodice.

Her mood was wistful and melancholy.

Frank sensed that right away. He knew that his primary responsibility was to ensure her comfort and safety, not talk her ear off, so he intended to zip his lips on the ride back.

"Please remember to put your seat belt on, and we'll be on our way," he said before closing the door.

Helen reached over her shoulder, pulled the belt across her upper body, and fastened it.

She set the gift bag next to her, laid her clutch on her lap, and rested her head against the cushioned headrest.

Her body was still pulsating, still deliciously tender and sensitive all over. And all she wanted to do was close her eyes, take a deep breath, and let her mind float back to Brenner and Irving.

Frank got in the driver's seat, and after closing his door, he looked at her through the rearview mirror.

"Excuse me, miss. Before we go, do you have everything? Do you have your little pocketbook?"

He was such the perfect gentleman, Helen thought. She couldn't have asked for a better driver.

Without opening her eyes, she said, "Yes. I have it." She touched it with her hand. She also reached inside the gift bag and touched the candle.

"And one last thing." He turned to face her. "No, two…" He paused and chuckled a bit. "And I won't bother you anymore. I promise."

Helen opened her eyes and met his. "You're not bothering me, Frank," she said, reaching for the hooks over her ears to remove the mask.

He smiled. "I set a cold bottle of water in that console for you back there." He pointed at it.

"Thank you. I appreciate that." Helen placed the mask inside the gift bag.

Frank nodded. "And the last thing. I'd, ah, be happy to change the radio station. Is there something you'd like to listen to?"

"This station is fine with me. Please…" She waved her hand. "Enjoy it because I'll probably fall asleep soon anyway," she said softly.

"Very well, boss lady. We'll be on our way." He locked the doors and put the car in drive. "Alright," he said, fastening his own seatbelt.

He glanced at her through the rearview mirror. Her eyes were closed.

I'll leave you to your precious dreams. He checked the side mirrors once more and then drove to the gated entrance.

He waved his hand at the security guard, and when the heavy metal gate swung open, he drove forward.

With her eyes closed, Helen heard the heavy clanking of the gate, which was in desperate need of some WD- 40.

When it closed behind them with a solid thud, she took a deep breath.

Frank glanced at her in the rearview mirror. "Traffic is light this time, so we'll make it back to the agency in short order." After saying that, he kicked himself, remembering that he wasn't going to talk her to death. Once they made it back to the Ree & Mosley agency, she would shower and change clothes before driving back home.

Hearing the gravel on the dirt road crunch underneath the car, she thought it was odd that an exclusive restaurant would be on a graveled road. "That's fine," she responded, not bothering to open her eyes.

As her mind flooded with memories and sensations tingled in her body, Helen Charlena Gothrock reclined against the plush leather seat and drifted off to sleep.

Chapter 8

HELEN PULLED INTO HER DRIVEWAY AT ten thirty that evening.

She pressed on the brakes and put her car in park.

Her cell phone was in the clutch bag, which was on the passenger seat. She reached for it and dialed Brenner's number.

"So, you're home safe?"

Just hearing his voice sent a soothing pulse through her like an aftershock.

"Hi, Brenner," she said softly, seeing his face in her mind. "Where's Irving?"

"Hello, my queen."

"Hi." Helen purred like a kitten.

"We've got you on speaker, my love," Brenner said, sounding as sexy as ever.

"I miss you both already." She looked at her house.

Helen and Walt lived in one of St. Winter's most exclusive gated communities. The other homes, like theirs, were beautiful brick mini-mansions with winding walkways. All the lawns were plush and professionally landscaped with colorful and seasonal flowerbeds.

A light was on in the living room and an upstairs bedroom; Walt would still be up, no doubt watching CNN.

Other than a pleasant hello, she wasn't up for any type of conversation with him.

I think I'll take a long, hot bath, and by the time I'm out, hopefully, he'll be asleep, she thought, gazing around her neighborhood.

Irving didn't try to hide the emotions he was feeling. "We miss you, too."

"Where are you?" asked Brenner.

"I'm still in the driveway."

"Helen, it's getting late. You should go in. Okay?"

"What if I don't want to go inside?" she said with audacity.

Brenner chuckled. "My little spitfire!"

She imagined him shaking his head at her boldness.

"Helen, Bren's right. We don't want anything to happen to you."

She knew she needed to go inside, but she wanted just a minute more. Even if she couldn't be with them in person, a connection over the phone would do.

It had been a long day. *A perfect, wonderful, and long day*, she reflected in the quiet of her car.

Frank had waited patiently while she had gone upstairs to the apartment above the garage, showered, and changed clothes.

"Miss, I'm going to follow you until you get to I-485," he had said.

"You've had a long day. You don't need to do that." She'd smiled, trying to convince him otherwise.

"Yes, I do. Besides, it's a man's duty to see to a woman's safety."

The finality in his tone had been clear.

Helen knew trying to convince him otherwise would be a losing battle.

The agency prided itself on seeing to every detail, and a client's safety was one of those details.

After giving him a bear hug and a kiss on the cheek, she said, "Frank, you are a true gentleman, and I cannot thank you enough for being with me today. Your level of service is unmatched, and I will definitely give you high marks when I speak with Ree and Maxx."

Helen gave Frank one more hug before getting in her car. And as he'd promised, he followed closely behind her all the way to I-485, which took her back to St. Winter.

Taking a deep breath, she said, "You're right. It is late. Plus, it's kind of odd for me to be sitting in the driveway this long." She chuckled.

She pressed the garage door remote, and as the door trundled up, she put the car in drive and eased forward.

"Good night, my love," Brenner said sweetly.

"Good night, Brenner." It came out as a near whisper.

Irving made a kissing sound. "Good night, my queen."

"Good night. I love you both."

"We love you, too, baby. Sleep well," Brenner said before ending the call.

She pulled into the garage and pressed the remote to close the door.

It was back to reality.

She turned off the ignition and unfastened her seat belt. Before going inside, she placed a call to Noel.

"Hey, girlie!" she said when her best friend picked up on the second ring. "Let's have breakfast in the morning! I've got lots to tell you!" Helen's voice was giddy.

Noel chuckled. "Where are you?!"

"In the garage. I just got home!" Helen said, sounding like a teenager sneaking in after curfew.

The overhead garage light went out, blanketing her in semi-darkness.

"It's ten thirty!" Noel laughed. "You left home at, what, ten this morning?!"

"Yes!" Helen giggled. "Can you meet me?"

"Hell, yes! I'll make reservations at Henry's for eleven. And why are you whispering?"

"I don't know!" Helen threw her head back and laughed, feeling so happy that she was lightheaded.

"I can't wait! I'll see you in the morning, slut puppy!"

"Slut puppy?! Why are you calling me that?!" Helen said, pretending to be offended.

"Don't play crazy!" Noel laughed. "If yo' ass is just getting home at ten thirty, y'all didn't just talk and have lunch! You fucked him, and don't act like you didn't!"

"We could've just had a good time, laughing and talking!" Helen chuckled.

"Like I said, see you in the morning, Miss Slut Puppy!"

Helen ended the call to the sound of Noel's laughter, and when she made it inside, she found Walt asleep with the news channel watching him.

Chapter 9

"LET ME GET TWO GLASSES OF CHAM-
pagne!" Noel said, smiling at the waiter. "Me and my best friend are
celebrating today! She's parking her car right now." She handed the
young man the drink menus.

"Got it." He returned the smile and tucked the menus under his
arm. "I've seen you in here before."

"Yes, we come here often." Her eyes brightened as she glanced
around at the other diners, many of whom she'd seen in Henry's lots of
times. The family-owned restaurant was a favorite spot in downtown
St. Winter.

The euphony of relaxed weekend conversations could be heard.
The aroma of fresh-brewed coffee and mouthwatering smells of food
wafted through the air as waiters hurried through the aisles, carrying
platters with fat Belgian waffles dusted in powdered sugar or generous
slices of thick-crusted quiche.

"Here are a couple of brunch menus. Take your time deciding what
you want." The waiter handed them to her. "But for starters, I'll get a

basket of muffins brought to your table. The blueberry ones just came out of the oven. They'll be nice and hot."

"Yummy! You guys have the best muffins!" She clasped her hands together.

Noel's stomach growled its impatience as a waiter walked by with a plate of bacon piled high over a mound of fluffy, farm-fresh eggs.

Helen came in and walked up to the hostess stand. "Good morning!"

"It's good to see you again, Ms. Gothrock!" the young woman said brightly. "I love what you're wearing!" She scanned Helen from head to toe.

"Thank you!" Helen glanced down at her legs. "I was thinking my shorts might be a little too short."

"Not at all," the hostess said, smiling. "You rockin' that!"

"Well, thank you!" Helen smiled. "I've got reservations, and I see my friend right over there." She pointed to Noel, who was tucked in a quiet corner booth. "Can I go on back?"

"Yes. Enjoy your meal."

As Helen stepped into view, Noel gasped. "Oh…my…God!" she said, cupping her hands over her mouth. She couldn't believe her eyes.

Helen had a wow factor, and her outfit put Noel's to shame. Noel glanced down at herself. She was dressed in a pair of boyfriend jeans, cuffed at the ankles, one of her husband's white dress shirts, which she'd tied at her waist, and a pair of leopard-print peep-toe mules. Her sandy-reddish hair was brushed straight back, and a pair of big gold hoop earrings hung from her ears.

But Helen was simply stunning.

Her pixie cut hair was combed into a side sweep, and a pair of white fringe tassel earrings hung down from her ears, so long that they brushed against her shoulders as she walked.

She was wearing a simple white ribbed tank top and a pair of stone-washed denim mid-thigh shorts that had her toned caramel-colored legs on full display. On her feet were strappy azure suede sandals.

But the "piece da resistance" that made her very chic was the long silk kimono she was wearing. It was in beautiful hues of vanilla, yellows, and summer-grass greens. Tiny sky-blue butterflies with orange-tipped wings and wispy frond leaves painted on the fabric gave the illusion of walking through a botanical garden. The weightless silk billowed behind her like a fan, lifting and floating in the airy breeze.

"Gorgeous," Noel whispered, unable to take her eyes off of her friend. "She's brand new."

Helen's skin was glistening, and she had an air of confidence and sexiness that seemed natural, not too much and not fake or phony.

Helen could tell people were watching her, and seeing Noel's expression made her want to laugh. She'd never felt so alive and free as her hips swayed to a rhythm of their own. She loved this feeling, and she hoped it stayed around for a long time.

"Oops!" Helen giggled and drew in a surprised breath. She halted.

Suddenly, from out of nowhere, a male waiter stepped in front of her and started singing and dancing circles around her.

"Yeah, yeah! Yeah, yeah! Feelings, so deep in my feelings. No, this ain't really like me... Listen to my heart go ba-dum, boo'd up..." He was singing Boo'd Up, by Ella Mai, a cappella.

As he started popping his fingers, cheers erupted at his impromptu *Dancing with the Stars* routine.

Helen threw her head back and laughed. She glanced down at the breast pocket on his uniform shirt. *Madison.*

She couldn't just stand there. *Why not*, she thought, joining in as a huge smile spread across her face. "Grab me by the waist, baby. Pull me closer…" After hearing the song on the radio enough times, she knew the lyrics well.

The old Helen would've shied away, graciously declining to be involved in anything like this, too constrained to indulge. But not today. She was no longer that woman.

Madison reached for her hand, and when she placed it in his, he lightly held it as they dipped their hips and twirled around to a boisterous rendition of the upbeat song.

Noel, like everyone else in the restaurant, laughed and clapped.

"…ba-dum, boo'd up…ba-dum, boo'd up…" Helen and Madison sang.

Several of the diners started singing along. "Ba-dum, boo'd up… ba-dum, boo'd up!" The excitement surrounding them was exhilarating.

Helen laughed, twirled, and dipped her hips, and when she glanced at Noel's face, she laughed even harder at her expression.

After a few more dips and twirls, Helen ended the dance. "This was so much fun! Thank you!" She threw her arms around Madison's neck and gave him a big hug. *He's handsome*, she thought, realizing that he could be no older than his early thirties.

Loud applause erupted, and they did a playful little bow.

"No, thank you, beautiful lady!" he said with a charming, flirtatious smile.

Her eyes seemed to sparkle. She smiled, waved, and looked around at all of the cheering faces in the restaurant.

When she reached their table, Helen couldn't help but laugh at the look on Noel's face.

"Girl, look at you!" Noel said, astonished at the transformation. "You look amazing!"

Helen laid her leather clutch bag on the seat and slid into the booth. Looking directly at Noel, she mimicked Ella Mai's British accent. "This is such a crazy feeling, though. I don't want to get too attached, but I feel like I already am…" She chuckled and gave her friend a sassy wink.

Noel heard a raspiness in Helen's voice, but before she could say anything, the waiter appeared.

"Excuse me. Your champagne. And for that performance of yours…" He paused as he looked at Helen. "The drinks are on the house. For both of you!" He smiled and placed a nearly full-to-the-rim flute in front of each of them.

"Nice moves, by the way!" he said, smiling at Helen.

"Thank you!" She grinned.

"And your muffins." He placed a basket covered in white tea cloth in the center of the table, along with two small plates and silverware. The aroma from the hot muffins was delightful.

"Thank you," the two women said in unison.

"I'll give you time to look at the menus and check back with you in a few minutes."

When they were alone, Helen looked at Noel and grinned. "Hello, my friend!" she said and then bit into a muffin.

Noel rolled her eyes. "Oh, no, Miss Thang." She watched Helen place a muffin on a plate for her. Leaning forward, she said, "I want details." She rested her elbows on the table and steepled her hands under her chin. "Talk, and don't leave out shit."

Helen laughed. "Damn, let me at least take a sip of my champagne first." She lifted her glass, feigning innocence, and took a sip.

Noel chuckled, picked up her flute, and did the same. "You straight?" She waved her hand towards the glass. "Now that that's out of the way, tell me how good he was, 'cause yo ass look like he fucked you real good."

Helen smiled as she took another sip. "This is some good champagne." She looked at the fizzing pops with interest before taking another bite of her muffin. "You need to eat your muffin while they're hot."

Noel rolled her eyes. "Don't ignore my question. Your voice is all hoarse like you've been screaming at the top of your lungs." She leaned forward and wiggled her finger, and Helen came closer. "Girlfriend, just how good was he?"

Helen smiled. "Why do you think I had sex?"

Noel rolled her head in a diva-esque way. "'Cause there ain't but one thing that will make you move and act the way you are. And that's good dick, and I mean real good dick. The kind that gets down in you and makes you move differently. Just like you switchin' down the aisle. Dancing and all. Don't deny it. Like I said, I want the details."

A mischievous smile spread across Helen's face as memories of yesterday flooded her mind. She looked at her friend. "You're wrong, Noel." She paused, letting a seductive tone creep into her voice. "Great sex with two gay men all day long will make you move differently, 'cause that shit is all the way down in my bones."

Noel's eyes widened in humorous surprise. "Damn!" She laughed. "Damn!" Lifting her champagne flute, she said, "I'd like to propose a toast to a woman I admire more today than I did yesterday."

Helen smiled and picked up her glass.

"Here's to one bad-ass woman who reclaimed the spark in her life."

They clinked their glasses, sealed the toast, and took a generous sip of bubbly.

Chapter 10

MEANWHILE, FORTY-FIVE MINUTES SOUTH of St. Winter, Irving stood above Brenner, who was sitting in a brown wicker chair on their screened-in porch.

The temperature was in the seventies. Except for a few passing clouds, the sky was filled with sunshine, and the morning was just right for an al fresco breakfast.

As his tongue eased into Brenner's mouth, he wondered, *Is this our one-millionth kiss?* Since they had bumped into each other that day at the Leisure Winery in Stoneville, the couple had been inseparable. It was truly coup de foudre. Love at first sight.

He couldn't think of a better man to spend the rest of his life with than the one whose arms were wrapped around his waist.

Moments later, Brenner ended the kiss. "You're trying to distract me from asking to help in the kitchen." He chuckled, looking both relaxed and sexy in his gray nylon jogging shorts and a thin short-sleeve zip-up nylon jacket in the same color. A five o'clock shadow framed his face.

"Bren, I told you already. I'm taking care of you today." A smile eased across Irving's face. "I know I said this before, and I know I'm going to tell you over and over." He paused before glancing out into the backyard. His hazel eyes settled on the rose bush, pregnant with deep red blooms. "What you did for me yesterday..." His voice trailed off as he turned and faced Brenner.

"What you did meant more to me than you'll ever know. I don't know how you did it, but you found me..." His mind searched for the right words as he saw Helen's face lying beneath him.

"Umph, umph, umph," he whispered, still feeling himself buried deep inside of her. He closed his eyes and took a deep breath. "You found me the perfect woman, and I will never forget what you did." He felt as if he were riding an emotional rollercoaster.

"You didn't judge me. Didn't get angry. Didn't question my love or my commitment to us. You just gave me what I asked for. No questions asked. You simply did it from a place of unconditional love. And I love you more than you'll ever know." His voice shuddered as his eyes glistened with unshed tears.

"So, Mr. Gary." He smiled. "Put your feet up on the ottoman and chill, my brother. Let your man take care of you today."

He turned and made his way to the kitchen. Stopping at the sliding glass door, he looked over his shoulder and winked at Brenner.

"Plus, I'm still floating, and my feet just won't touch the ground!" Laughing, he slid the door open and went inside.

As soon as he walked into the kitchen, a citrusy aroma hit him in the face. It came from all of the oranges that he'd juiced thirty minutes ago on their old-fashioned juicer. The juicer was a lone ranger amongst all of the modern Viking appliances.

They had spared no expense when it came to their home. Working with an interior designer, the couple had chosen shades of cream and gray accented with black, orange, and yellow for the color palette in their home. The kitchen was painted a light gray, with pops of yellow everywhere, like the decorative bowl of fruit on the breakfast table.

Earlier that morning, Irving had crawled out of bed, slipped on navy-blue jogging shorts and a lightweight blue cotton sleeveless hoodie and driven over to the corner bakery on East Boulevard in the Dilworth neighborhood.

The bakery had some of the best pastries in all of Charlotte, and he wanted them fresh out of the oven.

He had gotten an assortment of scones and muffins: buttermilk, cinnamon and blueberry and Brenner's favorite, morning glory muffins, filled with chunks of carrots, sweet raisins, coconut flakes, and walnuts.

He reached into the cabinet and pulled out two slender flutes.

"You're the one I want. You're the one I need..." he sang cheerfully as he poured the fresh-squeezed juice into the glasses, filling about a third of each.

He moved his hips side to side as he sang "Love on Top" by Beyonce at the top of his lungs.

Irving set the juice pitcher on the counter and made his way to the refrigerator. He grabbed the bottle of Naveran Cava, a sparkling wine, and the bowl with the sliced fruit.

The sommelier from Heaven, the Restaurant had given them the wine as a complimentary gift. The young man recommended sparkling wine for mimosas rather than champagne, sharing that it mixed better with juice.

With his hands full, he closed the refrigerator with his heel.

When he'd gotten back from the bakery, he cut up watermelon, strawberries, and honeydew melon and put them in a plastic bowl, and then he placed the bowl in the refrigerator.

He glanced at the coffee pot. Its aromatic aroma filled the air as the blended roast coffee percolated.

"Come onnn, baby, it's you…" *We're celebrating!* He thought feeling giddy, remembering yesterday.

He uncorked the cava and poured a generous amount into each glass, mixing it with the orange juice. "Oops, too much," he said, seeing some of the mimosa spill down the sides.

He leaned over and sipped a little from each glass.

With that done, he set the glasses on the tray. He'd already put two plates, napkins, and silverware on it.

"Almost ready," he said, placing the bowl of fruit on top of the stacked plates.

"You're the one I want…" he sang as he picked out a clean spoon from the dish drainer and stuck it on top of the fruit.

The pastry box was already on the wicker table outside.

Looking around, he was satisfied that he had everything. The sliding glass door leading to the screened-in porch stood open, making it easy for him to walk through.

"You got it?" Brenner said, coming to his feet.

"Yes. Sit down. I got it," Irving insisted, slowly making his way to the wicker table. "Remember, I don't want you to lift a finger all day today. I'm treating you. My way of saying thank you." He set the heavily laden tray down.

"Wow! This is quite a spread. I can get used to this." Brenner smiled and leaned forward.

"It's just muffins, scones and fruit."

"Which is perfect 'cause I'm still stuffed." Brenner chuckled, thinking about the food from yesterday. He rubbed his stomach.

"Me, too. Give me one second, and I'll get the coffee. It's not as good as Stine's, but it will do."

"Your coffee is fine, but make sure you bring your pretty self right back." Brenner winked.

Irving puckered his lips and blew Brenner a kiss before walking into the kitchen.

A moment later, the aroma of the steaming coffee blended with hazelnut wafted through the air as Irving came back and placed two cups on the wicker table.

He sat in the chair facing the backyard. "You know, judging from your expression and the way I feel, we must look like two lovesick puppies."

"I know what you mean. Helen was simply magical!" Brenner smiled before picking up his cup of coffee.

"I dreamed about her last night," Irving said as he scooped fruit onto Brenner's plate. "And yes, the only word to describe her is magical!"

Chapter 11

"YOU WANT ANYTHING ELSE?" IRVING asked, wiping his mouth with a napkin.

"Another mimosa when you get a chance." Brenner leaned forward and handed Irving his empty glass.

Irving set it on the tray. "Let me take this back inside, and I'll make you a fresh one," he said, stacking the dirty dishes, silverware, and coffee cups on the tray.

"You know, I can help," Brenner said, but he quickly laughed at the fake scowl on Irving's face. "Alright! Alright! I get it. I'm to do nothing." Shaking his head, Brenner waved his hand like he was waving a white flag.

"You're finally catching on," Irving teased him and looked around, checking to make sure he had everything. "I'll be back with your mimosa. I think I'll have another myself." He made his way to the sliding glass door.

"I was thinking we could get married in the backyard. What do you think?" Irving said as he glanced out at the yard. Their verdant lawn was like a sea of green, checkered with flowering bushes. "I think that spot over there would be nice." He motioned with his head towards the cluster of roses and zinnias that gifted the air with a delicate fragrance. The flowers would still be in bloom in September, which was the month of their wedding.

"I've been thinking the same thing," Brenner said.

"Give me a sec, and I'll tell you the exact spot where we can stand." Irving headed into the kitchen.

While he was inside, Brenner leaned his head back and closed his eyes. They had gotten in late last night.

"The rose bushes have a U shape," Irving said when he returned, and he handed over a fresh mimosa.

Brenner opened his eyes and reached for the glass. "Thank you."

"We could stand right in that open spot."

The rose bushes and cluster of zinnias had been planted in such a way that they formed a horseshoe. Standing in the center would surround them with a natural bouquet.

Lifting his glass high, Brenner said, "I love it! That's settled! Plus, it will save us money to have the wedding here, and the backyard is a decent size." He brought the flute to his lips and took a sip.

Their wedding would be an intimate gathering with forty of their family members and closest friends.

"I love the idea of getting married at home," Irving said, sitting down. He propped his feet up on the table. "Just think. Every time we sit out here, we'll be able to look at the spot where we became husbands."

Brenner nodded in agreement. "The moment I laid eyes on you, you became my husband."

"Baby, how sweet."

Brenner took another sip of his mimosa and turned to face Irving. "I've got to ask you a question."

"Ask me what?" Irving furrowed his brow before bringing the champagne flute to his lips and taking a generous sip.

"Are you good? Are you happy now?" Brenner said in a serious tone. "Me and you…" He paused and pointed at his chest and then Irving's. "We both know who we are, and I know, for me, I never thought in a million years…no, make that a billion years, that I would be with another woman. Yesterday was a head trip for me because I loved being with her. I can't lie. I know who I am, there's no question in my mind, but I've got to work through why Helen turned me on."

He chuckled. "Hell, maybe I've got some unresolved issues that I'll have to work through with my therapist. It'll probably cost me five thousand dollars just to find out that she was magical. Not figuratively, but literally." He shook his head and took a sip of mimosa. "So, let me ask you. How do you feel? Are you good? Are you happy?"

Irving looked at Brenner with an unreadable expression. He took in a long, deep breath as if giving himself time to gather his thoughts.

"Baby, my world was turned upside down yesterday. Not in a tragic way, but in an incredible, self-affirming way. You might not understand this, but I proved to myself that I was brave enough and loved myself enough to push past everything and do something that I truly wanted. Maybe even needed. Yesterday I let go and completely enjoyed the moment. You know, life is too short to miss those rare opportunities by staying in a comfort zone. Man, that took a lot of courage, but I didn't second-guess myself. I'm not second-guessing myself now. Hell, I know who I am. I'm the same man I've always been for the last fifty years. And if I live another fifty, I'll still be the same man who belongs solely to you."

A smile eased across his face, and unaware of the dreamy look in his hazel eyes, he glanced at Brenner.

"You asked if I was happy. Yes, I'm so happy and light that if I flap my arms, I will fly straight to the moon!"

The men shared a knowing smile, clinked their glasses and took a generous sip of mimosa.

Chapter 12

REE WONDERED IF HE WOULD VISIT HER
today.

She stood at the window and looked through the ornate scrolls
of ironwork, peering in her garden, looking for the friendly eastern
phoebe.

"Hoping to see that bird again?" Mary, the office assistant, asked as
she made her way into Ree's office. "I made you a cup of tea." She set
the cup on the desk and placed a coaster underneath it.

Every day for the past couple of weeks, the eastern phoebe had
perched on Ree's flowerpots and flitted through the tree branches, but
there was no bird sighting today.

Turning away from the window, she glanced at Mary. "What would
I do without you? Thank you for the tea." She pulled out her chair and
settled behind her desk. "And yes, I was looking for my little friend, but
with it raining outside, he might not show up."

"How do you know it's a he? It might be a she," Mary said
jokingly.

"It's definitely a male bird, and he's flirting with me." Ree laughed, picked up the cup, brought it to her nose, and breathed in the aroma. It was a black tea with carrot flakes, saffron, and natural Earl Grey flavors.

Leelynn Floyd, her best friend, had purchased several teas from Lula Carol's, a specialty tea shop located in one of Charlotte's most bohemian areas.

Mary chuckled. "I see. Well, you would know, Miss Matchmaker!"

"This smells wonderful." Ree blew a cooling breath over the rim before taking a sip. "Mmm, this is so good." She set the cup down before keying in the password on her computer.

"I hope Maxx gets a good report from his doctor today," Mary said, sounding optimistic.

"I'm sure he will. He's followed the doctor's orders the entire time. Plus, he's pretty healthy," Ree said, opening up her electronic calendar to peruse her call schedule.

Ree, along with her partner, Maxx Cousins, owned a private, ultra-exclusive dating service, the Ree & Mosley Agency. It was located in Charville, a small town thirty minutes southwest of Charlotte, near the McDowell Nature Preserve.

Part of the service included a follow-up call with each of their matched clients after the first date. If the dates were on the weekend, they conducted the calls on Monday.

They had found clients were most honest with their feedback right after the first date. This was the ultimate proof that the chemistry was right or wrong and confirmation that the match was a success or a failure.

Standing at the edge of Ree's desk, Mary bent over the vase of summer flowers and breathed in the delicate scent of yellow daffodils.

"Let me get back to my desk. Do you need anything before I go?" Mary said, making her way to the threshold.

Ree looked up, meeting her eyes. "No, I'm fine. It's just you and me today. Think we'll be okay?" She took another sip of tea.

"Not to worry. You know we got it!"

"I've got several calls today, starting at ten." Ree glanced at the clock on the wall. It was three minutes until ten.

"Would you like your door open or closed?"

"Please close it. I have a call this morning with the two people we matched recently. I want to find out how things went. In all the years I've been doing this, this match was one of those rare ones that don't happen every day!" Ree said, feeling butterflies in her stomach. "They both came into the agency on the same day. That has never happened. It was as if their destinies were intertwined, like the stars and the moons aligned to bring them together."

She inhaled. "I'll probably be on the phone with each of them for about forty-five minutes. No more than an hour."

"No problem. I'll hold your calls."

"Thank you."

Mary closed the door, and Ree was alone again.

"Ahh! Brenner and Helen!" She glanced at the clock. It was ten. "I'll bet we delivered on our promise. She dialed Helen's number. *Will I hear the vestiges of pleasure in her voice?*

On the second ring, Helen answered. "Hello! How are you!?" Her raspy voice beamed.

Ree's eyes widened, and she couldn't help but chuckle. Pleasure lingered in Helen's voice as thick as grits.

Chapter 13

"IT'S NOW OR NEVER," HELEN SAID.

She looked in the mirror one last time, straightened her shoulders, and took a fortifying breath. She smoothed down a strand of hair and brushed another behind her ear.

You's gotta see him sometime. Can't keep hidin'. It was the old-lady voice in her head.

The last couple of days, Helen and Walt had passed each other like ships in the night. Thirty-six holes of golf had kept him out of the house most of Sunday, and a bank merger meeting had occupied his time on Monday, well past nine that night.

Walt's absence didn't bother her; in fact, it suited her just fine. She hadn't been ready to face him, but it was inevitable.

"I've got this," she whispered. Convinced the bit of guilt in her stomach would dissolve, she clicked the light switch off in the bedroom.

She picked up her purse and briefcase by the door and made her way into the hall. *It's my life, and I can do whatever the hell I want.* She stepped into the kitchen.

He heard her footsteps.

"Good morning, stranger!" He smiled.

Things hadn't been right between them since she had shown him her boudoir photos, but deep down, he knew there had been an insidious crawl of unresolved issues that had brought them to this point.

"Morning." She glanced at him. A glacial coldness trailed in behind her like a shadow.

"Did you sleep well last night?" he asked as he set the paper down. He was sitting at the breakfast table, eating oatmeal and a slice of toast. His tall glass of orange juice and cup of coffee were hidden by the broadsheet of this morning's *Wall Street Journal*.

"Yes, I did. How about you?" She made her way over to the counter next to the butler's pantry and set her purse and briefcase down.

"I slept like a baby," he said, breathing in her rose-scented perfume, which tickled his nose.

"The coffee smells good," she said with a polite tone as she walked over to the coffee pot. Standing on the tips of her toes, she reached in the cabinet and grabbed her favorite demitasse cup.

He couldn't resist easing his eyes down her body as he watched her swaying hips covered by a pair of well-fitting navy-blue capri pants. Her top was a white knit sleeveless tank, and she wore a sheer navy poncho over it. On her feet were a pair of apple-green leather loafers with white tassels and blue topstitching, and diamond stud earrings sparkled from her lobes.

She felt his eyes and knew he was inspecting her and would find what she was wearing unsuitable for work. But what he didn't know was that everyone, including the executives, had all agreed to dress casually this summer.

She closed the cabinet, poured herself a cup of coffee, and stirred in a bit of almond milk.

"I left you some oatmeal, Lennie. It's still hot." He glanced at the pot on the stove. When they were in college, he'd started calling her Lennie or Len. That was his nickname for her.

"Thanks, but I don't have time to sit down for breakfast. I've got to rush out for a nine o'clock meeting."

She held the cup to her nose, breathed in the aroma, and blew a cooling breath. The smell of fresh coffee reminded her of childhood, when she'd watch her mother brew a pot for her father every morning before he left for work.

"I'll probably grab a bagel in the breakroom," she said, watching him over the rim of the cup.

Taking her first sip, she sighed. "This tastes great." She leaned against the granite counter, took several more sips, and gazed at him.

He was definitely the picture of money and success. He was dressed in black slacks and a black and white striped shirt. A perfectly knotted tie, made from the finest silk and with splashes of gray and green, hung from around his neck. Polished black wingtips were on his feet.

Too bad you're boring as shit and about as romantic as my left toe, whispered across her mind. But she had to admit, from the first time she'd lain eyes on him when they were in college, he'd been a good-looking man.

His brown eyes were so rich in color that she always thought of Hershey's chocolate. Light salt and pepper at his temples gave him a distinguished look, while a daily routine of working out for an hour had left him with a toned, masculine physique. Any woman would love to have his arms wrapped around her.

Walt smiled inwardly as he watched his wife's eyes trail down his body. "I've got to leave soon myself," he said, picking up the small container of cinnamon and sprinkling a liberal amount into his bowl.

He glanced at her. "Do you know if we have any raisins? I looked in the pantry and the cabinet but didn't see any," he said, stirring his oatmeal.

Giving him a casual glance, she sipped the last drop of coffee. "I don't know," she said plainly before placing her cup in the sink.

Walt bristled as if she'd hit him. *I'm sick of that fucking dismissive tone.*

"Dammit," he said. Letting out a breath, he lay his spoon against the side of the bowl. "What do you mean you don't know?" he said in frustration.

Ever since their blow-up at the dinner table where she smashed the mashed potatoes in his face, she had been rude, dismissive, and downright cold, and it pissed him off to the highest degree of pisstivity.

She glanced at him over her shoulder but continued washing her cup and dirty spoon.

"You're the one that keeps up with the food and goes to the grocery store. Hell, I give you the money to buy the damn groceries. What???" He paused, hunched his shoulders, and gestured with his hands. "Now I have to make the grocery list, too?"

She smiled at him, and when she didn't answer, tension entered the kitchen and stood between them like a third party.

"Helen?! What's gotten into YOU?" Walt snapped. "Are you still PISSED off because of my reaction to your photos? Damn! I apologized. Get over it!" he fumed.

He stared at her, clenching his back molars. "I was trying to be nice. I just asked you about raisins." He spoke with his hands. "And you give me a shitty response and look at me like you don't understand the words coming out of my mouth!" Trying to calm the rising heat of his frustration, he pinched the bridge of his nose and breathed in.

Helen had just climbed out of a self-induced rabbit hole, and with newfound strength and resolve, his moods no longer controlled hers.

She smiled. "Like I said, I don't know if we have any raisins." She placed the cup in the drain, dried her hands on the dishtowel, and walked over to the butler's pantry.

"I'll see you later." She picked up her things, turned, and looked into a pair of confused eyes. Not caring about the tension swirling around them like angry bees, she bid him a good day before closing the door.

"What the hell is wrong with you?" he whispered with unease.

Chapter 14

"YOUR DOCTOR GAVE YOU GOOD NEWS yesterday?" Ree stopped watering her ficus, which stood in a sunny corner, as Maxx maneuvered his wheelchair into her office.

She set the empty water canister on the floor by the planter.

"Yes, he did. Thank the Lord." He blew out an exaggerated breath. "Doc said my back has completely healed and this chair is unnecessary. Said I'm brand new." His smile conveyed his relief.

"So, why are you still ridin' around in that thing? You've become lazy and don't want to walk?" she teased.

"Something like that. By the end of the week, I'll put it in the closet in my guest bedroom." He set his laptop on the corner of her desk and booted it up.

She walked over, pulled out her chair, and took a seat. Then she opened the manila folder and glanced at the notes on the sheet of letterhead. She and Maxx needed to discuss the feedback received from the most recent matches.

"Maxx..." she paused and waited for him to look at her. "Since you're healed and brand new, maybe you'll ask Leelynn out."

He threw his head back and laughed. "Why are you all up in my business and hers? Don't you have anything better to talk about?" He unscrewed the cap on his bottle of alkaline water and took a generous sip.

She ignored him with a wave of her hand. "And before you tell me you don't find her attractive, you forget I'm in the matchmaking business! I know when two people have the right chemistry," she said adamantly. "And you all's chemistry is not only right, but also explosive. The kind where you rip each other's clothes off and just go at it! Go ahead, Maxx. Shame the devil and tell the truth."

"Okay, chem teacher, but remember, I'm not your client," Maxx said, but he thought, *Ree's spot on, 'cause Leelynn's the one I'd give up all these chicks for. And you're damn straight. If she lets me, I'm ripping all her clothes off the first chance I get.*

Ree and Leelynn had been friends since junior high. They'd graduated high school and college together, and as a graduation gift from their parents, they, along with a retired aunt and a cousin, had taken a year off and traveled throughout Italy before coming back home to Charlotte to begin their careers.

Ree knew Maxx hadn't been in a serious relationship in a while. And after Leelynn's break-up with her boyfriend a year ago, Ree knew her friend was cautious about getting involved with anyone—with one exception, Maxx. Leelynn had wanted him from the moment she'd met him, but neither had ever been free.

"You know, she has had a serious crush on you, and you've had a serious crush on her for a long time, too. You just chose to date a string of gold-diggers, and she ended up with a mama's boy."

"So, she likes mama's boys?" He couldn't resist.

"Of course not. She didn't know he was a mama's boy until she met his mother and she made it known that she didn't approve of Leelynn's natural hair." She chuckled. "Said it needed to be pressed or permed."

Maxx laughed. "I like her hair." A picture of Leelynn's face popped in his head, surrounded by her gorgeous, curly lion's mane. He liked more than her hair. In fact, he very much liked everything about her, and he had since laying eyes on her. But he followed one of his favorite mottos: when the time is right, it is right.

And he knew the time was right. Right now. Later that evening, he was calling Leelynn, but meddlesome Ree didn't need to know that.

"So, what did her boyfriend do, try to convince her to change her hair?"

"Exactly, plus his mother didn't like Leelynn's profession. She told her son that it wasn't right for a woman to take photos of other women in panties and bras for a living." Ree laughed.

Maxx chuckled and crossed his arms over his chest. "Let me guess. She told him to go straight to hell."

"You've got it! With gasoline drawers on his tail!"

They both laughed.

"Good for her! I thought she was a brilliant woman," Maxx said.

"Don't act like you don't like her, 'cause I can tell that you do!"

"Sis, like I said, I'm not your client." He took a big gulp of water. "I know how to get a woman. How to feed a woman…" He paused and licked his lips. "And I damn sure know how to satisfy a woman. So, stay out my business." He took another sip of his high-pH water. "You the one who has had a string of dates lately. You need to let me hook you up with Mr. Right! Let me match make yo' ass!" He laughed.

She drew in a surprised breath. Pretending to be offended, she threw a Post-It notepad at him.

"Maxx, shut up! You don't want me in your business, fine, and don't worry about my string of dates." She huffed. "I know what I'm doing. It's called research."

"Whatever, sis!" He leaned against the cushioned back of the wheelchair and crossed his arms.

She took a deep breath. "Come on, Maxx. You two would be perfect. Just ask her out."

Seeing her pouty lips, he chuckled. "Actually, I'm thinking about asking her to take boudoir photos of me. Maybe I'll wear black briefs and nothing else." He gave Ree a sexy wink.

"Spare me the visual, please." She rolled her eyes before picking up her cup and taking a sip of her now-tepid tea.

"What do you think? Black briefs or white?"

"About you in briefs?! I don't think nothing about that!"

He grinned. "You know, I could pull them down real low." He started nudging down the waistband on his slacks.

Ree covered her ears. "Stop! I don't want to hear this!" she said playfully.

He laughed. "I thought that would get your matchmaking butt off the subject."

She rolled her eyes. "Okay, okay. I'll stop for now. But..." She paused, wiggling in her chair with excitement. "I've got to tell you about my conversation yesterday with Brenner and Helen."

"That's right! You talked to them. I want to hear everything about our perfectly matched clients. Something tells me their date was sizzling hot!"

Ree nodded in agreement. "Maximus, we scored a triple home run with those two! I think they'll see each other again. Probably become a couple!"

He threw his head back and laughed. "A couple?!" His incredulous tone rang out loudly. "What you talkin' about? She's got to get rid of her husband first, unless she's just planning on having an old-fashioned affair."

"Helen doesn't strike me as the affair type," Ree said with assurance.

Maxx rolled his eyes in disbelief. "I don't know what you got in that cup, but it's making you hallucinate. You want some of my water?" He paused and swallowed a generous amount before leaning forward with the bottle in his outstretched hand, which she playfully waved away.

"The water might clear them cobwebs out your head, 'cause you need to stop acting like Helen is little Miss Goody Two-Shoes! You forget, Miss Thang came to us to go on a date with another man, knowing her ass was married. That's the makings of a woman who'll straight up have an affair. How you figure it ain't?!"

Ree smiled, she couldn't argue with logic.

Chapter 15

"MORNIN'," THE DELIVERY GUY SAID.

The receptionist pointed to the transaction counter. "Why don't you set them right here?"

He did as instructed and pulled the digital logbook from his shirt pocket. He swiped down the page, stopping at his first delivery for Friday morning.

"This is the CWF building, right? The Charlie William Foundation?"

"You're in the right place!" She laughed. "I would hate for you to have gone through this trouble only to be in the wrong building."

"You and me both!"

She smiled at his relieved expression.

"It says here the flowers are for a Ms. Gothrock." Pocketing the device, he gave the receptionist a courteous look.

"Oh! These are for Helen! I'll see to it that she gets them. Before you go, please type in your name and the name of your company." She pointed to the iPad mounted on the counter.

"Wow! This is quite an arrangement!" She chuckled. Flowers spilled over the sides of the vase in a riot of blooms. "Not only are the flowers gorgeous, but I can tell they're very heavy."

"Yeah, they are. Be careful picking them up." He sounded winded, as a sheen of perspiration dotted his forehead. Retrieving a handkerchief from his side pocket, he wiped his brow.

"I will."

"Also, her name is here on the card." He tapped the sealed envelope, secured by the plastic floral pick cardholder.

"Thanks! Have a nice day."

"Helen is going to love these flowers. What woman wouldn't?" she said, breathing in the fragrance.

Chapter 16

"YOU HAVE A SURPRISE!" MYIA GRINNED as Helen came down the hall towards her.

"What kind of surprise?!" Helen's eyebrows crinkled with curiosity. She reached Myia's desk and leaned against it.

Myia Jordin had been Helen's executive assistant for the last six years. They'd developed such a great working relationship that the women had more of a friendly mentor-mentee relationship. Myia had graduated from Bennett College in Greensboro, North Carolina, and was now studying for her MBA at the University of North Carolina in Charlotte.

"You'll see when you open your door!"

"Don't have me go in my office and end up looking crazy!" Helen gave her assistant the mean eye.

"I promise you won't!" Myia chuckled.

"Well, judging from the look on your face, it must be a good surprise."

"It is!" Myia shimmed like she had a big secret to tell.

"Alright," Helen said skeptically as she opened the presentation folder in her hand. Her office keys were inside.

"Your door is unlocked," Myia said, noticing Helen reaching for her keys. "By the way, how did the meeting go?" Myia pointed at the presentation folder.

"It went well." Helen sighed, "Two more later this afternoon, and I'll be ready to make a decision on which advertising company to hire to manage our social media footprint."

"Good for you. At least you've got a couple of hours before you have to go back in."

"That's right. Well, let me see what this surprise is." Helen turned to enter her office, but she was stopped by the expression on Myia's face.

"Now what is it, Ms. Jordin?! Why are you looking at me like that?"

"Oh, nothing!" Myia giggled like a schoolgirl.

"Ms. Jordin?" Helen gave her executive assistant a direct stare. "Tell me?!" She put her hand on her hip.

"It's nothing, really!"

"Then why are you smiling like that? You're thinking something. Spit it out!" Helen said with an impatient yet playful stare.

"Okay! Okay!" Myia said with an infectious laugh. Gesturing wildly with her hands, she took a deep breath and tried to control her fit of giggles.

"I'm just thinking that either Mr. Walt is making up for something or..." Myia paused, covering her grin with her hand.

"Or what?!" Helen raised her perfectly arched eyebrows. "You might as well say it, 'cause whatever it is, you're already thinking it!"

"Or..." Myia chuckled. "I'm just going to say it! Or you must be puttin' it down in the bedroom!"

"I'm not telling you my business!" Helen said playfully, but she thought, *Walt might be making up for his behavior, because we're definitely not puttin' nothing down in the bedroom.*

Myia Jordin smiled. "Yes, ma'am, boss lady."

Helen rolled her eyes. "Well, let me see what this surprise is." She opened the door.

Her eyes widened the moment her gaze landed on her desk. She drew in a surprised breath and, with a trembling hand, closed her door.

Chapter 17

IN THE MIDDLE OF HER DESK STOOD A huge crystal vase filled with a profusion of exotic black calla lilies. Queen Anne's lace had been perfectly arranged within the flower's white-speckled leaves.

"Oh my," she whispered.

Instantly she knew who the flowers were from. *We used this flower in some imaginative ways.* She chuckled, remembering just how creative they had been.

Today was Friday. Almost a full week ago, last Saturday, she'd had an affair and spent the entire day with two men whom she had fallen in love with. And while they had exchanged contact information, she hadn't expected to hear from Brenner and Irving again. She had only hoped.

Myia wouldn't come in her office without knocking, but Helen wanted to ensure her privacy. She locked the door and, on a pair of wobbly legs, made her way over to her desk.

With every step she took in her leopard-print slingbacks, her pulse raced, and a very luscious smile spread across her face.

She set the presentation folder down, bent her head, and brushed the tip of her nose across the bouquet's velvety petals, breathing in the soft fragrance of the purplish-black blooms, which she'd learned meant elegance and mystery.

"This has to be two dozen!" she said in awe. Using her index finger, she counted the number of flowers. She pulled one of the blooms from the vase, and tiny droplets of water ran down the stem.

Helen rounded the corner of her desk and sat, reclining her head against the cushioned headrest. Her eyes slid closed, and she blocked out the world and the sunlight streaming through the floor-to-ceiling mini blinds in her bright and airy office.

She'd take her time, think only about Brenner and Irving, and feel all over again the awakened sensations that tingled through her body.

Chapter 18

FIFTEEN MINUTES INTO HER REMINISC-
ing, the muffled ringtone alerted her to a call. She reached for her cell,
which she'd left in the presentation folder.

"Yes," she squealed softly upon seeing his number. She took a deep
breath, trying to calm the flurry of butterflies in her stomach, and
swiped right to answer the call.

"Hi, Brenner."

"Hello, my love."

Her heart skipped a beat hearing his voice. There was something
about it, with its deep, melodious richness, that reached inside of her
and twisted her insides, turning them mushy and gooey.

"I was calling to see if you got a special delivery."

"Yes, I did!" Her smile widened.

"Good! Glad they were delivered. Irv's going to call later. We were
going to call you at the same time, but he's tied up right now."

"I can't wait to talk to him. Brenner, the flowers are gorgeous, and
I love the Queen Anne's lace!" Her voice trailed off as she brought the
long-stemmed flower to her nose and breathed in its scent.

"Irving insisted on that."

"I thought so! They are lovely. How are you doing?"

"I've been good. No complaints, but I'm much better for talking to you."

"You're such a sweet-talker."

"Don't tell opposing counsel that." He chuckled.

"Absolutely not. Your secret is safe with me."

"Good deal. How have you been?"

"I can say the same. No complaints, and much better now that I'm talking to you." She swiveled her chair, stood, and made her way over to the floor-to-ceiling window. She looked through the slats in the mini blinds, down at the cobblestone streets of St. Winter and at the people walking up and down the sidewalks, living and enjoying their lives.

"Ahh, you're a sweet-talker!"

She chuckled. "What's all that noise in the background? You must be at the courthouse."

"Yeah, I am. The judge just gave us a twenty-minute recess. So, everybody's standing around. Let me walk over here to this window. It's further away from folks."

Dodging the people milling around, Brenner made his way to a corner window at the far end of the hallway. "Is that better?"

"Yes. Much better," she said; she could barely hear any of the previous noise.

He sighed. "I'm going to be here all day."

"That's what happens when you're the best lawyer in town."

Brenner chuckled low in his throat. "Am I the best, baby?" he teased, turning her words into a double entendre.

Lord have mercy. He sounds so sexy. "Yes, you are," she said sweetly as a tingling sensation eased through her.

"We miss you."

"I miss you all, too. Very much."

"So, tell me. What's my favorite lady wearing today?"

He was flirting with her, and she loved it. She glanced down. "Well, I'm wearing black linen capri slacks and a black short-sleeve knit top. A cowry shell necklace, a wide brown leather belt, and a pair of leopard-print slingbacks." Her tone was wrapped in a sultry heat. "How does that sound?"

"It sounds really nice, but what if I want to take it all off? Would you let me?"

"Only if you'll let me do the same to you."

"I wouldn't have it any other way." His voice was low and seductive.

"Can I ask you something…" Helen paused and lifted the flower to her nose.

"Anything. You know that."

"Please don't take this the wrong way."

"Not to worry. Ask away."

"So, are you guys into women now?"

Brenner let out a hearty, surprised laugh. "Not even the least bit! Don't get it twisted. We're only into you. There's something about you that drives me crazy. I haven't been able to put my finger on it yet. But one thing I do know is, you, my love, are magical."

"So, I'm magical?"

"Yes, you are! And you're gorgeous, sexy as hell, and a genius with a killer body."

"Ahh, so many compliments! I like!"

"Good. Because everything I just said is the truth. Let me ask you a question. Do the flowers bring back memories?"

"You know they do." Helen brought the flower to her nose and breathed in the familiar fragrance. "Brenner…" There was a soft longing in her voice.

"Yes, baby?"

"*Umph, umph, umph,*" Helen said under her breath as she made her way back to her desk. "I really miss you." She sighed wistfully. "I miss you both, and I've been thinking…" She paused. Pulling out her chair, she took a seat.

Sensing her hesitancy, he said after a moment, "You've been thinking what, baby?"

His words sounded like a serenade to her ears, and it gave her the courage to say what was on her mind. "I've been thinking that maybe we could get together again."

Nervous about his reaction, she stuck her pinkie finger in her mouth and bit her manicured nail.

The thought of having an affair used to be abhorrent to her. How a married woman or man could do such a thing was beyond her. But here she was, and the thought no longer felt abhorrent. It felt natural.

Helen heard his long sigh before he responded.

"Baby, I want that, too, but let me remind you of your obligations."

"What obligations?" She pretended a casualness.

"Ahh…" He laughed. "Let me help you out. I'll give you a clue. It starts with the letter 'h.' Does that help?"

"So?"

"So? What do you mean, so? Do you know what you're risking if you see us again?"

When she didn't respond, he said, "Helen, are you pouting?"

"No, I'm not." Her tone was tart.

"Yes, you are! You're pouting." He chuckled.

She exhaled. "He's not going to find out." Her tone was defiant.

"But baby, what if he does? My love, let's be real. What we did last Saturday was very special, and I loved every minute of it. But it was wrong. There's no two ways about it. We were wrong." His tone was firm and sure.

"At best, we could say it was in the heat of the moment. A one-night stand. Doesn't make it right. But if we get together again, that would be intentional, a deliberate act." His tone was matter-of-fact.

"First of all, I'm not interested in some 'intentional act' bullshit! We're not in a courtroom." She bristled. "And if you don't want to see me again, just tell me, counselor." Her feelings were bruised.

She threw the flower across the desk and crossed her arm over her midsection.

"I didn't say that, my love." He chuckled, and as he spoke, he sounded cool and measured. "We've got to think about this. Not rush into making any decisions."

"If you didn't want to see me again, why stir up my emotions?" The irritation in her voice was voluminous. "Why send me two dozen calla lilies?! That's no small gesture. Clearly, you knew that I'd know who they were from, and clearly, you knew I'd remember EVERYTHING we did that day. And why in the hell did you call me?!"

She rolled her eyes in frustration. "I just asked you an intentional and deliberate question. What's your retort, Mr. Lawyer?" Bitterness dripped from every word.

Brenner's laughter rang in her ear. "Ooh! There's my little spitfire! Remind me not to go up against you in court! Great argument!"

Helen took a deep breath and couldn't help but smile. "Don't give me some intentional bullshit, Brenner," she said, feeling less irritated.

"Alright, alright…" he said, still laughing.

Before he continued, he paused and took a breath. "But let's be serious. What if he finds out and wants a divorce? I'm not saying he'll go all the way, but it's a real possibility. Are you willing to risk your marriage? Think about it, Helen. Are you willing to do that?"

She took a deep breath and lifted her left hand.

The cushioned cut diamond in its platinum setting on her third finger caught the sunlight and sparkled, bouncing tiny prisms of light on the walls. She had always worn her ring with pride and a sense of accomplishment, but now it felt like a pricey reminder that her life was unfulfilled. A reminder that she wasn't happy in her marriage.

"I will if it means I can be with you," she said around the tender knot of guilt in her stomach.

"Let's think about this. Maybe take a couple of weeks to mull it over."

"I don't want to wait a couple of weeks."

Brenner sighed. "Helen, do you know what you're saying?"

"I know exactly what I'm saying, and who knows? Maybe we'll get together just once more."

After a very long pause, like the jury was out deliberating a case, Brenner finally spoke, "You know I'm a packaged deal?"

"Like I told you before, Irving only makes things more delightful and perfect."

"Are you sure, my love?"

"I'm absolutely sure that I want to be with you and Irving again."

He was quiet, and she could hear him thinking, weighing the pros and cons of what she'd asked.

"Brenner…?" she said softly.

"Yes, baby?" His voice seemed to have dropped an octave.

"When can I see you again?"

The sound of her voice wrapped around him so sweetly. "Irv and I have settled on September fifteenth for our wedding date."

"Congratulations!" she said genuinely. "Don't be surprised when you get a wedding gift in the mail from me!"

"Thank you! But you know what just occurred to me?"

"No, what?"

"Instead of you mailing us a gift, why don't you be the gift. Fly out to Maui. Join us on our honeymoon. I know that's several weeks away."

Helen drew in a surprised breath.

"We own a small house near Mount Haleakala. We'll be out there for three weeks, but I'm thinking it would be perfect for you to stay a week. Of course, I'll cover all of your expenses, including a first-class roundtrip ticket."

Twisting around in her chair, she looked at the calendar on her credenza and flipped to September. Except for the first week, her schedule was completely open. "I'm free practically the entire month."

His voice was soft and seductive. "Yes, you will be the perfect gift. How does that sound, my love?"

"Just wrap me in a bow!" she said softly.

Chapter 19

LATER THAT EVENING, AFTER WORK, HELEN wasn't ready to go home.

Agreeing to fly to Maui was a colossal size of wrong heaped on top of the colossal size of wrong she'd already done.

She needed time to reflect and anchor the bits of her emotions, which swung from guilt and remorse one minute to confusion the next, only to change a minute after that leaving her with an incredible feeling of sexiness and excitement.

Before leaving the office, she traded her leopard-print slingbacks for a pair of comfortable espadrille flats and sent Walt a text to let him know she was having dinner downtown and would be late getting in.

The temperatures had cooled, making it just right for a stroll, and St. Winter was gloriously bustling.

Strings of bistro lights were twisted around street poles, and summer flowers spilled out of box planters in front of the stores. People browsed in the shops, art galleries, and boutiques. Many were dining outside at the sidewalk cafes, and the sound of their laughter and conversations floated freely in the air.

Standing at the crosswalk, she smiled at the lady next to her, who was holding a toy poodle in her arms like it was a baby. The dog's snow-colored fur stood in stark contrast to its round black eyes.

Moments later, the light turned red, and cars eased to a stop. After looking both ways, Helen and poodle mom crossed the cobblestone street.

Helen continued on her way to Sisters Boutique, a shop owned by two sisters who had a bespoke collection of jewelry, skin-care products, home décor, fine chocolates, and fuzzy slippers. Oprah's magazine and *Vogue* had featured the shop in recent editions.

As she approached the boutique, she saw the elderly couple that she had met before, standing in front of the large display window, but it wasn't until she grabbed the antique brass door handle that their eyes met.

They were an amazing couple, she thought; love seemed to radiate around them like a visible aura. She smiled. "It's a pleasure seeing you again!"

"Thank you. It's nice seeing you again as well," the man said politely. A hound's tooth cap rested on his shiny bald head. "They have some nice things in this store." He glanced at her before turning back to the display.

"They do," Helen replied. Shifting her gaze, she watched him caress the woman's hand, nestled in the crook of his arm, as if he'd done it a million times.

When Helen glanced up, the elderly woman was looking directly at her.

"That's a lovely scarf you are wearing, ma'am," Helen said warmly.

"Thank you, dear." The woman's eyes sparkled with mischief as she brushed the silk fabric of her pink floral scarf. "You know, many things are said by a man's caress. And as long as you enjoy it, that is all that matters." She gave Helen a wink.

Helen's eyes widened. She hadn't expected to hear such a provocative comment from this matronly woman, and for a brief moment, she was speechless.

The smile on the woman's face suggested that she might be amused by Helen's reaction, and seeing that made Helen chuckle. *Where did that come from? It's like she knows something, but I like her! She's one sassy old lady.*

"Miss, we are going to be on our way. Have a good evening," the man said before gently shifting his wife away from the window.

"I wish you both the same." Helen looked at the woman and then the man. She wanted to talk longer to the elderly woman. There was something about her that broadcasted that an evening with her would be like an evening with Maya Angelou, a phenomenal experience. But she said nothing, letting the moment slip through her fingers.

"Take care," the elderly gentleman said.

"Thank you, and I hope you all have a good evening." Helen smiled and waved goodbye.

Standing at the boutique's door, she watched the elderly couple continue their evening stroll. The woman's words replayed in her head.

They gave her a sense of relief. She exhaled, and when she did, her emotional pendulum stopped swinging. "I'm definitely enjoying Brenner's and Irving's caress, and that is all that matters," she whispered to herself as she opened the boutique's door.

A tiny bell jingled above her head, and a rush of lemon-verbena-scented air enveloped her like a long-lost friend. She breathed in the scent, let it relax her, and smiled, knowing that with a pair of new fuzzy slippers, everything was going to be just fine.

Chapter 20

IT WAS SEVEN THIRTY THAT EVENING when Helen pulled into the garage.

After deactivating the alarm, she dropped the car keys, her purse, and the bag from Sisters Boutique on the counter by the butler's pantry door.

"Hey!" Walt said, coming into the kitchen with an empty wine glass in his hand.

She looked up, meeting his eyes. "Hey, how are you?"

"I'm good. I didn't hear you come in. I was upstairs watching the news," he said as he came towards her.

She smiled as her eyes eased down his body. He was wearing a light-weight black cotton bathrobe, tied loosely at the waist, and matching pajama pants.

Walt breathed a sigh of relief at her smile. He hadn't gotten many of those lately.

As he bent down and gave her a chaste kiss on the cheek, she smelled his clean, masculine scent, like he'd just taken a shower.

Her eyes also gazed at the soft midnight-brown hairs on his chest. She used to love nuzzling there, brushing the hairs from side to side with her nose, breathing in his scent. She thought it was one of the sexiest things in the world to do.

He took a step back and looked at the bag on the counter. "Did you have fun? I see you bought something."

"Yes, I did."

She slipped out of her espadrilles, and after leaving them by the door, she made her way to the stainless-steel refrigerator. "I'm thirsty."

"You want some wine?" He walked to the counter, where he pulled a McBride Sisters Sauvignon Blanc from the bottle chiller and poured some in his glass.

"No, I want water." She made her way to the fridge and pulled out a three-ounce bottle. With her back against the cold door, she opened the bottle and took a generous gulp. "That's good." She sighed as the water quenched her thirst.

"I left you some flounder on the stove. I stopped by Libby Hills and picked up two dinners."

"Thanks, but I ate while I was out," she said, meeting his eyes. "I'll put the food away before I go to bed."

She seems like she's in a good mood, he thought as he recorked the bottle.

He was making an effort to be nice because things between them were still not right. It was like walking on eggshells. He watched her body language for unspoken clues.

"How was your day?"

"My day was good. Yours?" She took another drink of water and glanced at the kitchen table, which was cluttered with today's mail and the morning paper. She walked over and looked through the stack. Finding a new catalog from Chicos, she picked it up and flipped through it.

"Oh, man." He let out an exaggerated sigh. "Super busy. You remember that bank acquisition we just made?"

"Yes, I do. Wasn't it Saini Bank and Trust?" She recalled the various conversations he'd shared with her over the past few months.

Work was all they talked about.

Let me go ahead and ask, he prompted himself. "Listen, umm…" There was a flutter in his voice, and before continuing, he took a sip of the white wine. Seeing the curious look on her face, he knew her ears had picked up that flutter.

"Walt, what is it?" She set the catalog down and guzzled the last of her water. Then she made her way over to the trash bin cabinet.

He took a deep breath. "I know it's late notice, but I've invited five of the bank executives and their wives over tomorrow evening around six for heavy hors-d'oeuvres and cocktails. I'll take care of the drinks, but I need you to freshen up the house and make some of that spinach and artichoke dip that's so good, maybe a platter of stuffed mushrooms and some of those sweet and sour meatballs that you make." He took another sip of wine. "And whatever else you think."

"You're right. It is late notice." She met his eyes. "Noel and I have booked a day at the spa tomorrow, and we're having a late lunch afterwards."

He drew in a sharp breath at her matter-of-fact tone. It pricked a nerve. *Dammit*, he thought. *She's going to dismiss me like that?*

Right away, she could tell that he didn't like her response, but that was his issue and not hers. One thing that she'd come to terms with was that, for years, she had prioritized his needs over hers.

She'd been the dutiful, mousy wife and enjoyed being the perfect hostess for his social/business gatherings, and she'd spent hours entertaining the wives and getting to know them. He loved showing off their home and his perfect life and marriage. She had always played her part, and she had played it well, all to make him look good in front of his business associates.

She was tired of playing that role. She'd played it willingly, but today was a new day.

He took a deep breath. "I know the timing's bad, Lennie, but I want to impress these people."

Leaning against the counter, she looked him in the eyes. "The house isn't dirty, but if you want to freshen it up, go right ahead. And while you're at it, prepare the refreshments and whatever else you want. I should be back by five or five thirty. Plenty of time before your guests arrive."

"Lennie…" He paused, "This is an important group of folks. I've already invited them, and they've made plans to be here." He set the wine glass on the counter.

His frustration was growing. In an attempt to relieve some of the tension gathering behind his frontal lobes, he pressed his index fingers against his temples.

"We've talked about this many times. You know how competitive and cutthroat the banking industry can be. One minute, you're on top, and the next, you're thrown out with yesterday's trash."

"Walt, I'm sorry. You should have checked with me first." Helen could see the strain growing in him and the tightness around his eyes.

"You're supposed to help me with things like this. You're my wife, Lennie…" He sighed loudly in frustration.

"Please, Len, change your plans. You can go to the spa anytime. Hell, I'll even pay for it." There was a sarcastic edge to his words.

She exhaled a deep breath as her patience was tested. "No, I'm not changing my plans. The next time, you should check with me first if you need my help."

She smiled, turned away from him, and walked over to the counter. Picking up her purse and shopping bag, she made her way out of the kitchen.

"I'm going upstairs to take a shower. I'll come back down and put the food away before getting in bed."

With an urgency in his voice, he stepped in front of her, halting her exit.

"Lennie, WAIT!"

Chapter 21

WALT SIGHED. "LOOK, I'M SORRY, AL-right? I know it's late notice. The next time, I'll check with you first." He paused…"But please help me out."

She looked at him. "Walt, like I—"

"I'm asking you nicely, Lennie." He said not letting her finish.

Judging from the look in her eyes, his pleas were not making a dent, and he blew out a frustrated breath. "What is it with you lately? You act like I bother you now. What's going on with you?" His temper was simmering.

"Like I said, I have plans tomorrow, but I should be back in time for your get-together." She stepped around him.

"Don't walk away from me. I asked you a question. What the fuck is going on with you lately?"

Without saying a word, she gazed at him with an air of indifference, or maybe she was challenging him.

He took a deep, calming breath and looked at her and her hair. Her loose curls were raked to the side in a casual style. She'd begun wearing it like this lately. She was also dressing and acting differently, becoming more and more a stranger every day.

"What am I supposed to do at this late hour?" There was a hopeful expression on his face. "Please, Lennie."

She shrugged. "Maybe call Southern Gourmet or Best Impressions or the country club first thing in the morning and see if they can cater something. Or go by Harris Teeter or Fresh Market and pick up a few platters."

He cocked his head to the side. Her devil-may-care attitude was beginning to boil his blood. "You expect me to do what?!"

"You heard me, Walt!!" She rolled her head dismissively. "I didn't stutter. And no, I'm not changing my plans. The house is clean, but again, if you want to freshen things up, run the vacuum cleaner."

Total confusion mixed with anger swept across his face, but he remained silent. *You've never spoken to me like this. What's really going on with you?* He searched her eyes for clues.

Taking a deep breath, he stood aside, letting her walk pass. *I don't know who you are.* Her disregard for him was real and palpable.

"I'm going to take a shower, read, and then go to bed."

"Sleep well, Helen," he sighed, and for the first time, he knew his marriage was in trouble.

* * *

The next morning, bright and early, Walt called the country club where he and Helen were members. He breathed a sigh of relief when he learned one of the lounge rooms was available. He reserved the room that was well appointed with plush cushiony chairs and couches. A bartender would serve drinks, and the club's chef would prepare trays filled with scrumptious appetizers.

All went well and everyone was very pleased, except Walt. As he watched Helen laugh and talk with the bank executives and their wives as if she had not a care in the world, he quietly fumed on the inside.

Chapter 22

IT WAS MONDAY MORNING, A SCHEDULED closed day for the museum, but Noel still opened the doors and instantly felt the rush of cool temperature-controlled air.

She flipped on the overhead lights, which cast wide ribbons of light across the highly varnished hardwood floors. The museum walls were painted a Benjamin Moore super white, the perfect shade for any art exhibit.

As the museum director, she curated the exhibits for the CWF Museum and led the administrative and operational functions. Most mornings, she started her day walking through in awe of the genius and creativity of the artists whose works were showcased. And today was no exception.

She had the space all to herself, and knowing that she was about to schedule her boudoir session, she couldn't think of anything more apropos than to be surrounded by paintings and collages by the phenomenal contemporary artist Mickalene Thomas.

Standing in front of a collage of a woman wearing a purple jump-suit, she admired the vibrancy of the piece as she pulled her cell out the side pocket of her emerald-green linen tunic and keyed in the number.

The tunic's three-quarter-length sleeves were rolled up, giving her a casual flair. Skinny gold bangles clinked and clanked every time she moved her arm, and a pair of ankle-length white jeggings and her favorite leopard-print mules completed her outfit.

She paced around, waiting for her call to be answered, and by the third ring, it was.

"Good morning!"

"Noel, it's a pleasure," Leelynn said. "From the wonderful things Helen told me about you, I feel like I already know you!"

Her infectious tone suits what she does for a living very well, Noel thought. "The same here! Helen's photos are so gorgeous that I decided I had to have a session! You're great at what you do, by the way!" She slowly made her way to the next collage.

"You're so kind! Thank you! I'm pulling up my July and August calendars right now. Let's see…" Leelynn paused. "With the exception of Mondays, what day of the week do you want to come in? I typically do not shoot on Monday. Oh, and do you want the same package as Helen?"

"Yes! She got to change three times. I want that as well." Noel squealed. "I'm so excited that I can't sit still!"

"I'm glad, and we're going to have lots of fun! So, what day of the week?"

"I think a Saturday," Noel said, brushing a strand of hair behind her ear. "I went shopping the other day, but I want to get a couple more things."

"Good for you! I recommend my clients bring more pieces than their package calls for. That way, we'll have choices. Plus, some things look different based on the lighting."

Leelynn scanned the month of July. A luscious smile spread across her face when she saw the twenty-eighth.

"My Saturdays book up quick. It looks like my next available one is August fourth at ten thirty. Is that good for you?"

"Perfect! August fourth, it is! This gives me two weeks to get ready and do a little more shopping!" Noel's voice radiated excitement.

"I've got you down! I'm looking forward to meeting you! Also, I'll email you tips and suggestions on what to do to prepare for your shoot. Expect the email right after this call."

"I'm looking forward to meeting you as well, and I can't wait!"

Leelynn's voice turned soft and sultry. "Before we go, let me ask you, are you ready to have photography, romance, and sensuality twine around vous?"

Noel had made it to another painting. This one was of a woman with a big afro and wearing purple lipstick. It was hard to miss the beauty, boldness, and voluptuousness of the woman looking directly at her. This was how Noel felt at this moment.

She smiled and said, "Yes, Leelynn, I am absolutely ready for all of that to twine around me!"

Chapter 23

THE FOLLOWING THURSDAY, BRENNER and Irving tasted cakes in a pink stucco bungalow in the Dilworth neighborhood, a historic community minutes from uptown, that was filled with huge old trees with thick trunks and long, stretching limbs.

The bungalow was home to Miss Loretta's Cake Shop.

Loyal clients came from near and far for her legendary cakes, which tasted like a slice of heaven. She was a childhood friend of Irving's grandmother, which had earned him a spot on her loyal client list years ago.

Miss Loretta was an older black woman who usually wore a tie-dyed tignon around her head, which she knotted in the front, giving her a regal look. Today the tignon was purple and mint green, matching her white, purple, and green cotton maxi dress.

Inside the bungalow, the living room had been converted into an open and airy space. Instead of traditional furniture, there were several large glass display cases along the walls, showcasing her cake designs. Four vintage rosewood Victorian chairs were available for guest seating.

On a nearby buffet table sat a fresh pot of coffee, an old-fashioned tea kettle, silver tins with loose-leaf tea, and bottles of water. Closest to the bay window, an antique desk and chair were set up as the sales transaction area.

The dining room, aptly called the Tasting Room, had a large, oblong table with six chairs around it. Guests would taste cakes and frostings until they found their irresistible combination.

"Babe, we've got to decide," Irving said, licking the last drop of surgery sweetness from his spoon.

They'd taken the day off, along with Friday, hoping to finalize many of the details for their wedding.

"This is yummy! I want this cream cheese buttercream frosting." He laid the spoon on the terrycloth towel.

"Perfect!" Brenner smiled and giving him a thumbs-up. "And the three-layer Meyers lemon is my top pick for the cake. Agreed?"

"I couldn't agree more!" Irving said, watching his soon-to-be husband place a big checkmark by *select cake* on the to-do list.

Leaning over to Irving, Brenner smiled. "You've got a little bit of frosting on your lip. Let me help you out." He added his own bit of frosting as he gave Irving a sweet kiss.

Moments later, he pulled back. "*Umm*, that's good."

Miss Loretta had been watching them. "You know…" She paused as a broad smile lit up her oval face.

Looking first at Irving and then Brenner, she said, "I'm going to find some stardust to mix in the cake batter, 'cause I've never seen a couple more in love than the two of you. You fill me with such joy. I wish you both Godspeed." She blew them a kiss.

"Thank you, Miss Loretta!" Irving smiled and glanced at Brenner before pushing back his chair. "I like the sound of stardust! Give us lots of it!" He stood.

He was dressed in a pair of tan linen Bermuda shorts with a black polo shirt tucked inside. A black leather belt, accented with a gold buckle, circled his waist, and a pair of vintage checked Burberry leather slide sandals were on his feet.

Miss Loretta stood and walked around the table. He stretched out his arms, and she stepped into his warm embrace.

"Irving, I'm so happy for both of you," She said affectionately.

"Thank you!" He kissed her forehead, feeling her sentiments tug on his heartstrings.

"Yes! Thank you so much!" Brenner stood behind the older woman and wrapped his arms around Irving's shoulders, sandwiching the petite woman between them. He gave her a gentle squeeze.

"We also want you to come to our wedding," he said as he eased back. He was wearing khaki Bermuda shorts, a simple black leather belt, a white dress shirt with the sleeves folded up, and a pair of well-worn black leather loafers. "And bring a guest. Maybe a hot date!" He winked at her and watched as she walked to the head of the table.

She picked up her cup of coffee. "What do you mean, a hot date?!" She scrunched up her eyebrows as she brought the cup to her lips and took a sip.

"Now, Miss Loretta, as fine as you are, you know plenty of men are interested in you!" Irving smiled.

"Oh, I've got lots of old men clamoring for my attention..." she said in a sassy tone. "But you said a hot date, not an old date!" She laughed, and the sound was rich and full like family members laughing together at a reunion.

"Well, get you a hot young man. Be a cougar!" Irving teased good-naturedly, as he high-fived Brenner.

"Yeah, right! The only young man I know is my grandson, Trey. He's twenty-five. The girls think he's hot." She chuckled and rolled her eyes. "Quite frankly, I don't get it."

The men looked at each other, and in silent agreement, Brenner said, "Well, just for you, Miss Loretta, bring both. Your young man and one of your old men. How about that?"

"I just might do that! But send me a proper invitation. Put mine in the mail."

"Yes, ma'am!" the men said at the same time.

"None of that texting or emailing stuff."

"Absolutely not! You will receive your invitation by US mail. Not to worry," Irving assured her.

With their cake order confirmed and the delivery date and time set, Brenner paid the deposit.

Standing at the door, it was time for goodbyes.

Miss Loretta stood on the tips of her toes and gave Irving and Brenner a motherly kiss on the cheek. "I love you both, and I'm praying for your marriage. May it be a good one that is long and filled with health and wonderful and intimate moments that take your breath away."

As the two men made their way to the car, both knew they'd treasure this unforgettable time spent with Miss Loretta. She was now a part of their wedding memories.

Chapter 24

IRVING'S HAZEL EYES ROAMED DOWN the face of the man who meant more to him than air.

Brenner's love had given him the space to feel stable and steady, the space to heal and grow, and after fifty years on the planet, he had learned to treasure himself.

"Give me some sugar," he whispered as he leaned across the plush black leather seat of Brenner's late-model Jag XJL.

Moments later, after easing his tongue from Irving's mouth, Brenner said, "*Mmm*. How's that?" He settled in the driver's seat.

"Just what I needed!" Irving smiled. Bringing the strap of the seat belt across his body, he clicked it in place.

Brenner started the car, and the engine roared. He clicked his seat belt, adjusted the A/C, and put the car in reverse. "Before I Let Go," by Maze, featuring Frankie Beverly, played softly through the car's Meridian sound system.

He backed the car out of the driveway and pulled onto the street. Quaint houses in pastel shades of green, yellow, pink, and light blue dotted the street. Gingerbread lattice stretched along the gabled roofs of some.

As they drove along, Irving gazed out the window. He pulled out his cell phone, went to his contact list, and dialed Nyoni Couture in uptown.

"What's up, man?!" he said when Nyoni picked up after the second ring, "We're headed your way."

He and Brenner had been shopping at the upscale men's clothing store on North Graham Street for years.

"Ask him if he's going to be there," Brenner said, briefly meeting Irving's eyes.

Irving nodded and said into the phone, "Bren wants to know if you're going to be there. We can't leave our tuxedos to just anybody!" He laughed. "Got to get that right!"

After a moment, he glanced over at Brenner, "He'll be there." Then, into the phone, he said, "Okay, cool! We'll see you soon." He ended the call.

They spent the next two hours getting fitted for tuxedos. While they did, they sipped champagne, nibbled from a charcuterie board filled with sliced turkey, ham and pepperoni, white cheddar and brie, baby carrots and hummus, green olives, fig jam, and an assortment of nuts and dried fruit.

They also laughed a lot and added the time getting their tuxedos to their wedding memories.

Chapter 25

AT TWENTY-FIVE MINUTES TO ONE, THEY left Nyoni's.

Brenner suggested they walk the two short blocks to the florist rather than hop back in the car.

As they stepped outside, the roar of cars driving by, horns honking, and sirens blaring in the distance greeted them.

"Hopefully, it won't take long to pick out the flowers and our boutonnieres," Brenner said.

"I already know what I want us to get, and after that, we can go to this little sandwich shop that Stine told me about and have lunch. It's on the same block as the florist."

"Cool. Plus, I'm ready to eat something more substantial than what we had."

As they continued walking, Brenner noticed a few gray clouds had formed. "Let's hurry our pace. It looks like it's going to rain." He glanced at the sky.

"Rain is good," Irving said before smiling at the woman walking towards them, holding a little girl's hand.

Brenner gave the woman and girl a cordial nod.

"So, tell me, my dear, what type of flowers do you want?"

Irving smiled. "I want lots of white and lavender chrysanthemums. They remind me of perfectly shaped bouquets. I want flowers everywhere!" He talked with his hands. "In the yard, in tall planters, and some on the grass. I want them throughout the house, too! And I want huge bows in white and burgundy satin ribbons tied around the base!"

Brenner chuckled as he gazed at his partner. "Sounds like you've been giving this a lot of thought."

"I have!"

"If that's what you want, that's what we'll get. I have no problems with that," Brenner said as they made their way down the sidewalk.

"You give me everything I want." Irving gave his partner a sexy wink.

"That's right! What about our boutonnieres? I'm sure you have already decided," Brenner teased.

"I have!" Irving smiled. "If we can still get them, I want grape hyacinths and a red rose. You know why?" He glanced at his partner.

"Of course I know! We met at that vineyard in Stoneville that had those muscadine grapes. I was minding my own business, and you started flirting with me!" Brenner laughed.

"Is that how you misremember it?" Irving said, rolling his eyes in a diva-esque way. "But if you didn't have selective amnesia, mister, you'd remember that you were flirting hard with me. I remember correctly that you couldn't take your eyes off my fine ass!"

"You're exactly right. I couldn't take my eyes off of you then, and I can't now!" Brenner said proudly.

By one forty, the couple had selected the exact flowers that Irving wanted, paid the deposit, and confirmed the delivery date and time.

They left the florist and walked the short distance to the sandwich shop. By the time Brenner opened the door, the clouds had darkened, and big drops of rain were falling from the sky.

Chapter 26

IT WAS A LITTLE, OLD-FASHIONED SHOP
with a quaint mom-and-pop atmosphere.

Dark wooden tables were draped in plain white tablecloths. Green and white striped curtains hung from the windows, simple artwork adorned the clean white walls, and a working jukebox in the back corner played the latest song that someone had paid twenty-five cents to hear.

A young woman with a cheery disposition walked up to them. "Good afternoon. Welcome to Bamboo's!"

Irving and Brenner smiled. "Two for lunch," Brenner said.

"Right this way." Her toothy grin showed a mouthful of braces. She led them to a quiet corner table.

Her blackish-brown hair with blue ends was twisted into a messy bun, and a tiny diamond stud sparkled from her nose piercing.

"We've heard great things about this place," Brenner said. He pulled out the chair facing the door and sat down.

"Yes, we have!" Irving looked around, pulled out his chair, and took a seat. "I'll have to thank Stine for the recommendation."

Several diners sat at the other tables, which were spread through-out: an older couple in their seventies, an athletic guy who looked like a football player or fitness buff, and a family of five.

She smiled pleasantly. "Thank you! I'll tell my uncle. He owns the place." She laid two leather-bound menus in front of them.

"What's good here?" Brenner asked.

With youthful exuberance, she smiled. "Well, we're known for our hot teas and muffuletta sandwiches! My uncle prepares them with lots of capers, thin slices of pickled cauliflower, and an olive spread that contains his secret ingredients."

"A culinary genius!" Irving said, meeting her eyes.

"And our teas are really good, too!" She pointed to the tea menu, a single sheet of cream-colored parchment paper on the table.

"The mint tea is my fav! While the water is boiling, he flavors it with these herbal sachets that he makes..." She patted her chest. "*Mmm*, it's yummy."

"Irv, I don't know about you, but I'm sold! A muffuletta sandwich and mint tea for me." Brenner handed her the menu.

"Same for me!" Irving chuckled. "If I get anything else, I'll probably want to eat half of his!" He nodded his head in Brenner's direction.

"No, no!" She waved her hand. "You should look at the menu first!" She laughed. "I didn't mean to persuade you! My uncle will kill me!"

"Nope! Our decisions are made!" Brenner teased.

She smiled. "Okay! Great choice, if I must say so myself. You're going to love it! Two muffulettas and two mint teas, coming right up!" She took the menus and left.

Alone again, Brenner got his partner's attention by brushing his finger across the back of Irving's hand. "We made it just in time." He said, looking out the window.

Irving glanced over his shoulder and watched as sheets of rain came down. It was pouring outside.

"I've got a question for you." Brenner stared into a pair of eyes that felt like home, looking for any uncertainty. "Are you good with me inviting her to join us in Maui? It'll only be for a week."

Irving took a long breath. "You know, at first, I was super excited, but after thinking about it, I'm not sure I want her there. Don't get me wrong. I fell in love with her just like you. But truthfully, I only wanted to be with a woman one time. I shared you once, Bren, and I don't want to do it again."

Brenner caressed Irving's hand again. Rarely did they show affection in public. And while brief, the simple stroke was a tender reminder of their intimacy.

He exhaled at the serious look on his partner's face. "You know my priority is to make you happy, and if you don't want her there, I don't want her there."

"I don't need or want anyone else other than you," Irving said. "But let me ask you a question. Is this something that you want? We're going to live the rest of our lives together, and I don't want to worry that she owns a part of you. Do you have latent needs that I should be concerned about?"

They were getting married soon, and Irving didn't want to go into his marriage wondering if there was more to Brenner asking Helen to join them. He didn't think so, but he needed the reassurance.

Brenner leaned back, brushed his hand down his face, and sighed heavily.

A brief silence drifted in before he opened his mouth. He had been doing a lot of deep thinking about Helen, specifically his reaction to her. While he'd enjoyed the moment and loved every minute of it, there was nothing in him that needed to be with a woman.

"Let me say this. The only needs and wants that I have are for you, and there should be no doubts in your mind. It's just that we had so much fun and we all fell for one another."

"I get it," Irving said, "and she asked to see us again. Although I suspect she really wants to see you. I'm not stupid. But check this out. She can't have my man." Irving cocked his head to one side. "No more! She had you once, and that's all she's gon' get."

Brenner reached for Irving's hand. "I will figure out how to tell her that Maui is off. I'll come up with a nice way."

"Be very nice. She means the world to us. I don't want her feelings hurt. Let her down easy."

"No worries. I'll be the perfect gentleman."

"Good. Because she can't have what is mine."

"I've got it!" Brenner chuckled. "One thing I love about you, Irving Holmes, is that you don't have a problem telling me exactly what's on your mind. And let me make sure you know what is on mine. You own my heart and my body. You never have to question who I desire. It is and will always be only you. I am yours just as you are mine."

Irving smiled. "I love you, Brenner Douglass Gary."

"I love you more."

They turned as the young woman approached.

"Perfect timing," Irving said.

"Be careful. This is hot. Just let it steep for another minute." She placed the white porcelain teapot in the center of the table. Then she removed two cups from the tray and set them on the table, along with a small mason jar filled with honey. Packs of sugar were already on the table.

"Thank you," the men said almost at the same time.

"Your sandwiches will be ready shortly. Enjoy." She walked away.

"You smell that?!" Brenner asked as steam rose from the porcelain spout like a warm, minty greeting.

Irving bent forward and breathed in the aroma. "Yes, I do!"

"Well, well, well! Who do we have here!"

Damn, Brenner thought when he saw who was approaching their table.

Chapter 27

THE WOMAN WAS DORISSE GLENN.

Her entitled and flirtatious tone wrecked the mood instantly.

I'll be damned, Irving thought as he glanced up at her. Drops of rainwater adorned her perfectly coiffed hair.

Brenner sighed and gazed at her. *The day was going so well. Now we got to deal with you.* "Mrs. Glenn," he said politely. Irving kicked his shin under the table.

"Fancy running into you all in this quaint little place!" she said with a temptress's smile. She rubbed her bejeweled hands together to dry them.

Casually dismissing Irving, she focused on Brenner. She looked at him like he was a must have.

Help me, Jesus. Irving groaned inwardly at her outlandish boldness.

"How are you?" Brenner asked cordially, ignoring her wanton gaze.

Dressed in her usual St. John and low-heel, patent-leather Ferragamo shoes, which were drenched, she stood out in the little sandwich shop like a neon sign.

"Please, call me Dorisse," she said, batting her mascara-coated lashes behind the tortoise-shell glasses perched on the bridge of her nose.

She glanced at Irving before turning her attention back to the man of her interest.

"Sorry, but my parents taught me to respect my elders." Brenner could tell she didn't like that comment.

"Well...age is but a number," she said in an admonishing tone. "But since you're being formal, I will do the same. How are you, Mr. Gary?" Her tone was as sassy as ever.

"I'm doing well, ma'am." Brenner met her eyes and then folded his arms across his chest.

"I'm just tickled pink that I ran in to you!" She said, her eyes roaming freely over his face and the diamond stud sparkling in his earlobe.

Looking around the restaurant, her nose in the air, she said, "I'm only in here because it's pouring down outside; otherwise, I wouldn't be here. But it looks like the rain is my friend today!"

She smiled and turned towards Irving, "And you, Mr. Holmes? How are you?"

"I'm good, Mrs. Glenn." Irving's tone was dry, and he resisted the urge to roll his eyes.

Dorisse was in her mid-seventies. As one of the wealthiest dowagers in North Carolina, she was a huge philanthropist and sat on several boards, including the A. Pearl Academy, where Irving served as chair. She was also known as one of the city's biggest flirts, and she had no problem paying men for their company, especially in bed.

Irving kicked Brenner under the table again and chuckled when he winced. "I think the tea is ready." He picked up the porcelain pot and poured a stream of amber-green liquid, filling Brenner's cup and then his own.

"Thank you," Brenner said. He picked up the honey and stirred in a bit before handing the mason jar to Irving.

"Well, Mrs. Glenn…" Brenner said, but he stopped when the young waitress approached.

They all turned in her direction.

"Ma'am, your table is ready," she said, motioning for Dorisse to follow her.

Dorisse put her finger up. "Thank you, dear. Give me just a moment, and when I'm ready, I'll let you know." She turned and faced Brenner.

"Mrs. Glenn, you should probably be seated before this place gets crowded. Several people have already come in, no doubt due to the rain."

"Yes, I will, Mr. Holmes," she said dismissively. "But Mr. Gary, you were about to say something before we were rudely interrupted."

Irving sighed and blew out an exaggerated breath.

This is one crazy lady! Brenner thought, fully aware of Irving's recent encounter with her during their last board meeting.

Brenner smiled, cold like ice water. "What I was about to say, Mrs. Glenn, was that we want to have our lunch in private and bid you a good day."

Dorisse smiled and put her hand on her hip. "Bid me a good day?" She cocked her head to the side, and with a shift in her stance, she leaned down towards Brenner.

"I know how you can bid me a good day." Her inner sex kitten was on full display. "Agree to spend it with me in bed."

Chapter 28

"HOW DARE YOU!" IRVING GLARED AT her, his eyes widening at her audacity. *You bitch*, he said under his breath.

Dorisse looked at him. "Oh, I absolutely dare!" she said in a dismissive tone.

She was the type of woman who felt she could have any man. And while, to some, she might appear desperate, Dorisse wasn't desperate at all. Far from it. She was a woman who'd grown accustomed to saying and getting whatever she wanted.

And she didn't believe in coincidences. Rushing into the little sandwich shop just to get out of the rain and seeing the object of her desire was a sign to proceed. Straight ahead, without caution.

Brenner held up his finger in a manner that got Irving's attention. "I've got this," he said sotto voce, giving his partner a wink.

Irving rolled his eyes, exhaled, and picked up his tea. He blew a cooling breath over the rim before taking a sip.

"You just name your price, Mr. Gary." She brazenly licked her lips. *This is one good-looking man*, she thought, anxious to run her hands down the contours of his dark- chocolate face and broad chest.

"Name my price?" Brenner's tone feigned confusion. "What do you mean?" he said before taking a sip of his tea.

"You're teasing me. I like that."

She was a beautiful woman, but her wealth had given her the courage to be reckless, and it had lured many men to her bed.

"Let's not beat around the bush. We're both busy people. You know exactly what I mean." She smiled. "I'll pay you five thousand dollars for one hour of sex. But if you require more, just tell me."

"Ouch!" Brenner yelped.

Irving had kicked him, harder this time, and it earned him a direct stare from his partner.

Brenner sighed. "Five thousand dollars?"

"Money talks, and I've got plenty of it." Dorisse eased her eyes over his upper body.

Irving kicked him again.

"Would you stop?" Brenner glared at him.

"I'm not sure what the two of you are doing," she said looking back and forth between the two men. "But yes, five thousand dollars for one hour of sex. And if you stay the night and have sex with me repeatedly, I'll give you fifteen thousand." Dorisse slowly brushed a strand of hair behind her ear.

Irving coughed. "Damn! Fifteen thousand!" He snickered.

"That's quite a sum of money, Mrs. Glenn." Brenner smiled. "Fifteen thousand dollars?!"

He glanced at the young woman heading their way with the tray of food. "Give us a moment, please," he said to her, holding up his finger.

"No problem. Just let me know when you're ready." The young woman turned and walked away.

"Let me get this straight," Brenner said, steepling his fingers. "In front of my partner, who's sitting here as a witness, you just offered to pay me five thousand dollars to have sex with you for one hour. Is that right?"

Dorisse batted her eyelashes. "That's right! I see you're smart and good looking."

"Or fifteen thousand if I stay the night and have sex numerous times. Is that right?" Brenner asked, knowing his temper was growing as his patience dwindled.

"Yes. That's correct. I know what I want, and I'm not afraid to go after it. And I want you, Mr. Gary!" she said with hubris.

She puckered her lips and did a little shimmy with her hips. "I'm dead serious. I want you to give me hot, passionate sex all night long, and I'll pay you fifteen thousand dollars."

"Again, let me get this straight," Brenner said, veiling his growing irritation. *Surely, she can find a man without stooping this low. Hell, I know a few clients I could introduce her to if she wasn't so damn arrogant.*

Dorisse's sultry tone softened her chuckle. "That's what I'm trying to do. Get you straight." She winked at him before glancing back at Irving, who just stared at her with a penetrating gaze.

Bitch, he thought before taking another sip of tea.

"I see. So, you want to make me straight. Is that it? 'Fix my gayness'?" Brenner said, using air quotes.

"Yes, but truthfully, I just want to be with you." Dorisse put her hands on her hips and waited for his response.

Brenner gazed out the window. Rain pattered against the glass, and a clap of thunder boomed. He was quiet for a moment, as if contemplating her request.

He breathed in and rubbed his hands down his face. He met her bold eyes before looking at Irving.

"Babe, Mrs. Glenn has just offered to pay me five thousand dollars to have sex with her for an hour. And if I have sex with her throughout the night…" His voice trailed off as his eyes freely roamed down her body. "She'll give me fifteen thousand. Is that what you just heard?"

"Yes. That's exactly what she just said!" Irving winked.

Brenner swung his attention back to her. "Is that right, Mrs. Glenn? You're offering me five thousand dollars for one hour of sex, or fifteen thousand if I have sex with you repeatedly? And if I want more than that, all I have to do is name my price? Is that correct?"

Coming closer to his face, she breathed in his cologne and nearly swooned from his masculine scent.

"That's exactly what I said. I'll pay you five thousand for an hour of sex or fifteen thousand for a night filled with hot, passionate sex!"

She's so arrogant that I doubt she even hears herself, Brenner thought, taking a sip of his tea.

"Ahh, that's good." He set the cup down and turned to face her fully.

Crossing his arms over his chest, he said, "Mrs. Glenn, are you aware that in the state of North Carolina and all of the states in this country, with the exception of Nevada, propositioning someone to have sex for money is a criminal offense. And by you offering to pay me five thousand, or even fifteen thousand, to have sex with you repeatedly is nothing more than prostitution and punishable by one to five years in prison."

Dorisse drew in a surprised breath. "Don't you…know…know who I…am? I have friends who are law…lawyers and judges!" she fumed. "They'll run circles around you!" she added bitterly.

With a calmness that had won him countless courtroom battles, Brenner looked Dorisse dead in her eyes. His contempt for her was evident in his tone. "Now, if you don't want me to bring charges against you for prostitution and rip your reputation up one side and down the other, you apologize to Mr. Holmes." He glanced at Irving before turning his attention back to her.

"Wh...at! What do you...you mean?" she stuttered as her eyes swung back and forth between them.

Brenner gave her the facts. "I'm sure the ordeal would be quite a spectacle and, no doubt, every detail splashed across the front pages of the *Observer* and every other newspaper and media outlet in the state. Even if your judge friends and your pocketbook keep you out of jail, I'm pretty sure your board opportunities and invites to social events will dry up overnight."

The veins in her neck bulged. "How dare you!" She was fuming. *Doesn't he know who I am?*

Her breathing grew more rapid with every breath. *The nerve!?*

"You'd be the laughingstock of the city. After all, no one wants to be associated with a prostitute, Mrs. Glenn," Irving said, and he watched that sink in.

Her eyes bulged behind her glasses, giving her a comical look, and Irving coughed to stifle a laugh.

Brenner glared at her. "You apologize to Mr. Holmes for disrespecting him. And don't you EVER speak to him or me in this manner ever again, or I will be forced to file a lawsuit against you. And while you're at it, keep my name out of your mouth," he said angrily.

Dorisse huffed. "You...you don't tell me wha...what to do!" Her face flushed. "Don't you know who I am?!" She was fuming, but she felt like ice-cold chills were running through her body.

Brenner leveled his gaze at her.

"My partner and I have suffered you long enough, and the unmitigated gall that you've shown, one, to think that you could buy my sexual favors, and two, to be so rude and disrespectful to make this foolish request in front of my partner, who is the most important person in my life, quite frankly makes me sick to my stomach." His voice was colored with disgust.

Embarrassment chiseled away the confident, arrogant lines in her face, which were as much a part of her as her cheekbones, lips, and nose.

"I'm waiting. You apologize. Besides, we're ready to eat our lunch and get back to enjoying our day, and nowhere in the scenario does it include you."

She stood there like a frozen statue.

Brenner slammed his hand on the table as his anger overrode what little patience he had left.

"NOW, Mrs. Glenn!"

Dorisse jumped at the volume and harshness in his voice.

Chapter 29

HUMILIATION SWEPT THROUGH DORISSE with such force that she could barely stand.

I'd be a spectacle. Everywhere I'd go, people would point at me. Laugh at me behind my back. This isn't how I want to live my life. She had never felt so dumb in her entire life.

Withering like a vine on a tree without roots, she dropped her head in shame. *Mae told me to leave them alone, and she was right. I should've never approached him, and I had no right whatsoever to assume that he'd want to be with me. Now I've stepped into a pile of mess that I've created.* She fidgeted with the hemline on her jacket.

She sighed, thinking, *But I've got to fix this*, and when she did, remorse was written all over her face.

Dorisse took a deep breath as her face flushed. "Mr. Holmes and Mr. Gary..." She paused. Swallowing what little bit of pride she had left, she met their waiting eyes.

"I'm an old woman who has behaved badly and foolishly. And I..." She looked fully at Irving. "Mr. Holmes, I sincerely apologize for disrespecting you. You are a wonderful man and a brilliant board chair.

The A. Pearl Academy is fortunate to have you. I hope you can find it in your heart to forgive this old woman."

"I accept your apology," Irving said with a slight nod.

"Thank you," she whispered.

"And Mr. Gary…" Dorisse turned and faced him. "Mr. Gary…" She took a deep breath, hoping the infusion of air would steel her spine. "I apologize to you as well for my disrespect and inappropriate request. I beg of you to please accept my apology. I will never speak to you in this manner again."

Brenner was ready to accept her apology. He knew it had taken a lot out of her to simply say these words. He pushed back his chair and came to his full height. Standing in front of her, he extended his arms.

She stepped into his embrace.

As he wrapped his arms around her shoulders, giving her a gentlemanly hug, she felt it was an olive branch, a consolation of sorts, and she gladly accepted his gesture.

"Mrs. Glenn, yes, I accept your apology."

He stood back and looked down into her eyes. "And as far as Irving and I are concerned, we will never speak about this matter again, and I trust you will do the same."

"You have my word," she said softly before taking a deep breath. "While I do not agree with your lifestyle, I imagine you don't agree with mine, either…" She smiled. "But I now see the love you have for each other, and it's beautiful. Thank you both again for accepting my apology. I will commit to my word. Don't you worry. I won't speak on what transpired today ever again. And Mr. Gary…" Dorisse inclined her head in his direction. "I will keep your name out of my mouth."

She lightly tapped the table. "I will let you get back to your meal. And before I forget, congratulations on your upcoming wedding. I wish you the best, and if you don't mind, it would be my honor if you accept a gift from me."

"Mrs. Glenn, not that you have to get us anything, but we will gladly accept your gift," Irving said, touching her hand.

"Thank you." She smiled. "I will definitely get something nice, and with that, I bid you a good day."

As she made her way to the door, Dorisse glanced back over her shoulder. *I wish I had someone who looked at me with the same adoration as these two.*

She squared her shoulders, took a deep breath, and walked out into the pouring rain.

Her black umbrella was no match for the downpour, but it didn't matter. She'd throw away her ruined clothes and shoes, schedule a hair appointment the next day, buy a new umbrella, and set her sights on another man.

Chapter 30

LATER THAT DAY, LEELYNN WAS FINISH-
ing up in the studio. While her client was getting dressed, she thought
about Maxx. He was unlike any man she had ever dated, and he was
the only man she truly desired. Whenever she was around him, her
world felt right.

Several days ago, he had called and invited her to his place for
lunch this Saturday. Although he had been released from his doctor, he
was limiting his driving to traveling between work and home.

As she put away her camera equipment, her mind drifted back to
their conversation.

"The time is right for us, Leelynn, and I think you know it, too. I
would love for you to come over and let me cook for you. Would you
like that?"

"Yes," she'd said instantly.

"I'll have one of the chauffeurs pick you up."

"No, Maxx. I'll drive. You're not that far from me."

"Are you sure? Because it's no problem getting a driver."

"I'm sure." There was a slight pause before she continued. "Maxx, what are we going to do?"

"I just want to lay up with you, baby," he whispered like he was telling her a secret. "Feed you grilled shrimp, Mexican street corn, and iced tea." Like swaying palm leaves, his tone was smooth and easy. "And be lazy all day, kissing on you, sucking on your toes, and licking your fingers. Will that be alright, Lee?"

"Yes, it would," she murmured as her eyes slid closed. The way he talked to her and looked at her made her feel like a flower petal floating in a breeze. Light, beautiful, and soft.

"I want you to spend the night so I can wrap my arms around you while we sleep and then wake you up with my kisses."

She moaned, feeling warm and lush as he seduced her.

"Will you let me do that? 'Cause I can't wait any longer to be with you."

"Yes, Maximus, you can do all of that as long as I get to wrap my arms around you and kiss you," she said softly, hoping he heard the longing in her voice.

"You can do anything you want, baby," he whispered.

Chapter 31

LEELYNN GLANCED AT THE CLOCK ON the bathroom counter. It was ten. She had another hour before leaving for Maxx's. She wanted to arrive by noon.

Last night, she'd taken her braids down and washed her dark copperish-brown hair, combed coconut oil through her wet curls to condition and soften them, and left her hair to dry on its own.

Before she'd stepped out of the shower, she had shaved her legs and under her arms and exfoliated her skin with a sweet-cream sea-salt scrub. And while her skin was still damp, she'd scooped out a generous amount of vanilla-bean whipped shea butter and massaged it all over, leaving her entire body, even the tips of her toes, glistening and silky smooth.

Standing at the vanity mirror, she picked up the bottle of Kiehl musk oil, poured a few drops in the palm of her hand, rubbed her hands together, and started oiling her hair.

As she looked in the mirror, she shaped and fluffed her loose curls so that they framed her face like a lion's mane. Her soft hair was full, curly, and long, like the famed diva Diana Ross. As she worked her fingers in her hair, the towel around her body slipped down a bit, but she didn't bother to adjust it.

A couple of minutes later, she finished with her hair, and now it was time to get dressed. She had already washed her face and moisturized it with a light almond oil. Tossing the pink towel across the tub, she flipped off the light switch and closed the bathroom door.

She loved pink. The quintessential feminine shade always made her think of romance and peonies.

As she made her way into her bedroom, from the corner of her eye, she saw the white sheers on the windows lifting and blowing like a bride's veil from the air coming out of the vent directly above them.

When she'd decorated her bedroom, shades of pink, white, and gray had been her choices to go with the well-loved antique pieces that had been owned by her grandmother, like her four-poster canopy bed with white sheers looped around the posts, so long that the fabric pooled onto the gray carpeted floor. In a corner by the window was a contemporary pink suede tufted French chaise lounge. A gray chenille throw lay at the foot.

Leelynn spent hours here, sipping tea or drinking wine while reading her favorite novels and magazines.

She reached the side of the bed.

"Alexa, play 'The Secret Garden,'" she said while looking down at her dress, undergarments, and jewelry lying on top of the covers. Her undergarments were by LaPerla and in a beautiful black silk with ivory frastaglio lace embroidered on the delicate edges.

"Playing 'The Secret Garden,' featuring Barry White, James Ingram, and El DeBarge," the cloud-based virtual service said in her British accent. Soon the bass voice of Barry White filtered through the speakers.

"Okay, I got to get moving!" Leelynn clapped her hands excitedly. She picked up her panties and stepped into them. Next she slid her arms into the bra straps and reached around her back to hook the snaps.

With that done, she walked over and sat down at the antique mirrored dressing table that was in another corner of her room. It, too, had belonged to her grandmother.

She opened the top-right drawer. Inside was her makeup: NARS brushes, eyeliners, tubs of mascara, eye shadows, under-eye concealer, and MAC lipsticks.

While looking at her reflection in the mirror, she carefully applied her makeup. Not much. Just a sweep of eye shadow, liner, mascara, and a little under-eye concealer. She used an eyebrow brush and pencil to define her brows. And lastly, she put on her lipstick, Paramount by MAC. It was a reddish-brown shade.

"Lovely!" She smiled at her reflection in the mirror and then glanced over her shoulder at the clock on her nightstand. It was ten forty-five.

"I've got a few more minutes," she said, picking up the big gold hoop earrings. She slid the posts into her ears and pushed the tiny closures on the back to secure them.

With that done, she walked back over to the bed and picked up her dress, a white, silk-cotton blend in a men's shirt style with scalloped sides. She slid her arms in and buttoned only the middle five buttons, leaving lots of her pretty bra exposed at the top and generous amounts of her silken thighs to peep out with every step she took.

Next she rolled and cuffed the sleeves up until they stopped just below her elbows. Then she slid on two chunky gold bracelets. Every time she moved her arm, they clanked rhythmically.

"I'm ready!" She patted her stomach, feeling the fluttering butterflies nervously bouncing around on the inside.

Walking back over to the dressing mirror once more, she assessed herself from head to toe, and she loved what she saw.

She left her bedroom and made her way downstairs, her bracelets clanking with every step.

On the couch in her living room lay her overnight bag and purse. Her cork braided mule stilettos were on the floor, and she stepped into them.

With the sun shining on her face and a luscious, sultry smile on her lips, she gathered everything in her arm and set the alarm. As she closed the front door, her pulse raced just thinking about the one and only Maximus "Maxx" Cousins.

Chapter 32

IT WAS NOON.

After her hour-long workout earlier that morning, Helen had showered, washed, and conditioned her pixie-cut hair, brushed it straight back, and left it to air dry.

She'd finished eating lunch and made her way into the sunroom, with a mug of cold-brewed coffee in one hand and a romance novel in the other.

The only things on her Saturday agenda were to be lazy and relax.

She set the coffee on the small side table and took a seat on the white wicker settee with green and white striped cushions. She tucked her legs underneath and got comfortable before taking a sip of coffee. "That's good," she said with a sigh.

Taking a deep breath, she settled back and opened the novel, *Indigo*, a historical romance by Beverly Jenkins, one of her favorite authors. She had read the book many years ago, but every now and then, she'd reread books that she loved.

Thirty minutes into her reading, she heard the faint sound of the garage door opening. Walt had made it back from playing golf. He'd left around six thirty that morning.

Moments later, he padded through the house as he made his way into the sunroom.

"Hey," he said, looking sun-weary and drained.

She chuckled. "You look worn out!" She glanced down at her book, dog-eared the page, and set it next to her.

Barely glancing at his wife, he plopped down on the settee next to her. He crossed his arms over his stomach and laid his head back as if it were suddenly too heavy to hold up.

He let out an exhausted breath. "I am!" He turned his head towards her and eyed her dress. He hadn't seen it before and thought she looked sexy as hell in it.

She was wearing a long, strapless light-blue maxi dress that accentuated her toned arms.

"It's no wonder." She saw the sheen of perspiration on his forehead, "I bet it's at least ninety-nine degrees outside. How'd you do?" She watched his chest rise and fall with his slow, restful breaths, and then she eased her eyes down his body.

He was dressed in a pair of tan shorts and a white polo shirt. His feet were bare, which meant he had either left his golf shoes and socks in the garage or by the butler's pantry.

"I came in second!" was his breathy response. Although he was bone tired, his deep-rooted confidence colored his inflection.

"Well, good." She reached for her coffee and took another sip.

"Let me have some of that." He inclined his head towards the mug.

She handed it to him and waited as he took a big gulp. "Ahh, this quenches my thirst." Handing the mug back to her, he gave her a slow, sexy smile.

"You look pretty," he said, noticing that she was wearing little makeup with the exception of clear gloss on her lips and black mascara on her lashes. She had a natural beauty that he loved.

"Thank you." She felt her heart skip a beat as a twinge of guilt pricked her, knowing that she was having an affair and that, just two weeks ago, she had spent the entire day with two men.

Walt's smile was so sexy, though, and it had been a long time since she'd seen it. It felt like a lifetime ago, and she couldn't deny the immediate tingling that it caused. But she averted her eyes to avoid that smile and started looking at the tall planter in the corner by the window.

Until the guilt dissolved, her eyes traced the feather-like green fronds on the fern, and then she busied herself by gazing at the vase of fresh-cut daisies that sat on the wicker coffee table.

"I'm starved." He shifted onto his right hip and leaned towards her. "What did you cook?" From his vantage point, he eased his eyes over the top part of her dress, seeing her slightly hardened nipples through the fabric.

She took a deep breath, brought the mug to her lips, and swallowed, hoping to soothe her guilt. Setting the mug back on the table, she picked up her book and opened it to the marked page.

"I didn't cook anything," she said in an unbothered tone as she casually brushed back a strand of hair, unaware that when she did, the bodice of her dress slipped down to reveal the top swells of her breasts.

"I made a salad and ate some of the leftover spaghetti. There's plenty in the pot on the stove."

"Lennie, you know I don't like leftovers."

She met his eyes. "If you don't want spaghetti, there's lots of food in the refrigerator. I'm sure you can find something to eat," she said, not looking away from him.

It had taken her years, but she'd become fluent in reading his body language, his unspoken thoughts, and when his nostrils flared, she knew what he was going to say.

He exhaled, his short temper fueled by exhaustion and hunger. "I don't want to come home after being out all day and have to find something to eat," he said, throwing her words back at her. "It would be nice if my wife had enough sense to cook." He sighed audibly. *Damnit, I shouldn't have said that.*

He rubbed his hand down his face. *She's sitting up here, looking at me like she could give a rat's ass. She knows I hate leftovers,* he thought, trying to calm down.

He sat up straight. "Helen, I'm sorry for saying that, but I'm hungry, and I'm tired. Do you mind preparing me something to eat? Please?" His tone was congenial.

She met his eyes. They always reminded her of Hershey's chocolate. She eased her gaze down his handsome face, noticing that the sun had kissed his skin and darkened it just a bit.

He askin' you nicely, the old-lady voice said, her voice ringing with laughter. *Go on and fix him somethin'.*

She had been hearing this voice in her head for years. While it always spoke the truth, there were times she pretended to be deaf. And now was one of those times. She untucked her legs and crossed them at the ankles.

"Like I said…" She paused and glared at him, "There's plenty of food in the refrigerator. All I want to do is relax. I've had a busy week, and right now, I don't want to stop what I'm doing to prepare you something to eat." She glanced down at her book and picked up where she had left off.

What the fuck?! he thought.

And in that split second, the air between them thickened, becoming an invisible, noxious fog.

Chapter 33

WALT AND HELEN WERE SITTING SIDE BY
side on the white wicker settee. Inches separated them physically, but
emotionally, miles were between them.

She was calm to the point of being aloof, and he watched as she
read her book like he wasn't there.

He breathed out slowly and rubbed his hands down his face. He
needed to get a grip, and as though he were playing a game of internal
wordsmithing, he carefully thought about what he wanted to say. He
wanted to avoid the mistake he'd made earlier.

"May I ask you a question?" he said, noticing a robin flying near
the sunroom windows as if it were peeping in on them.

"Yes, you can, and since when do you need to ask for permission?"

"Well, I feel like I'm on shaky ground," he said, feeling out of
sorts. He couldn't believe she was holding a grudge. This was so unlike her.

"So, what's your question?" She laid her book across her lap.

"Are you still mad for my reaction to your photos? Or is it the
pictures I had on my phone? Is this why you've been so angry with me

lately? Even though I apologized, I feel like nothing I do or say is right. What is it?" He gestured with his hand as he spoke.

She took a deep breath and picked up her mug. "Walt, actually, I'm over that," she said before draining the last drop of coffee, "but I have to admit that I've taken a good look at a lot of things, and it's been eye-opening for me."

Her acerbic tone wreaked havoc on his attempt to be patient, and his eyebrows furrowed. "Eye-opening? What does that mean?" He shook his head.

She smirked. "Let's just say it led me down a different path." Brenner's and Irving's faces swept through her mind; the memory of them was so fresh she could still feel them.

"I'm going to ask you one more time. What does eye-opening and a different path mean? What are you talking about?" he said in a challenging tone.

She ignored his questions and instead decided this was the perfect moment to go in the kitchen. "I'm going to get some more coffee. Would you like a mug as well?" She got to her feet.

He was deeply angry that she had dismissed him again. *If you're going through some sort of midlife crisis, you better hurry the fuck up and get over it because I'm not taking too much else from you.*

He let out an exhausted sigh. "You know what?!" He paused and massaged between his eyebrows. His demeanor had turned brutally serious. "I'm getting real sick and tired of you, Helen. And I'm too hungry to sit out here and play twenty questions with you or try to figure out what you mean. I asked you a question, and I'd appreciate an answer, if that's not asking too much."

His stomach decided this was an opportune time to growl.

She glanced down at him. "I'm going to get some coffee." She took a step around the wicker table.

With a look of raw arrogance, he grabbed her hand. "DO NOT WALK AWAY FROM ME!!" The volume in his voice was loud, and the force of his tone was as sharp as a knife blade.

She felt the pressure of his hold like a vice grip, and her pulse began to race, but she refused to cower.

"LET GO OF MY HAND!" she yelled and snatched her arm away.

His temper began to boil, and he stood. As he loomed over her petite frame, his eyes bored into hers, holding them captive.

Their conversation had gone from bad to worse, and the little robin who flew back and forth outside the sunroom windows was an eyewitness.

Chapter 34

MAXX LIVED IN THE TRUST CONDOS, ONE of Charlotte's most sought-after addresses.

It was on S. Tryon Street, a tony neighborhood minutes from Uptown. Professional football players, basketball players, and some of the city's wealthiest entrepreneurs also called this place home.

His two-bedroom, two-and-a-half-bath unit was contemporary. It had an open floor plan and was airy and spacious, with varnished hardwood floors, exposed ductwork, white quartz countertops, and a wall of glass that gave him panoramic views of the skyline. It also boasted a rooftop terrace that gave residents a private oasis amidst the city's hustle and bustle. As a great cook, he loved the state-of-the-art kitchen that was equipped with everything he needed.

With Ree's help, he had decorated with black velveteen and rich taupe leather furnishings with splashes of teal and gilded gold. A zebra-print rug was in the foyer and great room, and original art hung on his walls.

Earlier that morning, his housekeeper had spent over two hours doing a deep cleaning of every nook and cranny, and she'd changed the bed linens and dusted.

While the housekeeper had done her thing, he'd prepped the food for their lunch and dinner by washing and chopping vegetables, seasoned the shrimp and chicken, and prepared the rub for the corn. He'd also made the tea, lightly sweetened it, and left it cooling on the counter in the kitchen.

When the condo was spotless, he'd paid the housekeeper and gotten ready himself, and just before leaving the bathroom, he'd poured several drops of oud cologne in his hands and rubbed the rich, smoky fragrance over his face and neck and on his wrists and hair.

Since he and Leelynn were staying in, he'd dressed casually in a pair of cream-colored linen drawstring pants and a cream and brown striped linen short-sleeve shirt, which he'd left unbuttoned.

He glanced at his watch. It was eleven fifty-five.

As he made his way through the condo, he breathed in the scent from the sweet plum and sandalwood incense and decided to light a few hurricane candles on a silver tray in the front room. The tangerine flames flickered from the gentle flow of air from the ceiling fan.

At exactly noon, the concierge rang. "Mr. Cousins, your guest has arrived. Shall I send her up?"

"Thanks, and yes. Please show her to the elevator." Maxx took one last look around, picked up the remote to turn on the sound system, and then pressed the button to lower the white mesh shades on the floor-to-ceiling windows, creating a soft sepia tableau just for her.

Chapter 35

LIKE OPPONENTS STANDING IN A BOX-
ing ring, Helen and Walt stared at each other.

Annoyance filled his chocolate eyes, and defiance filled hers as their marriage tumbled like brittle tumbleweed down a steep hill.

He breathed in. "I'm asking you again, what the fuck does 'taking you down a different path' and 'eye-opening' mean!?"

She heard the hungry growl coming from his gut, but she ignored it and concentrated instead on the anxious butterflies fluttering in her stomach.

Squaring her shoulders and steeling her spine, she didn't temper her tone. "Don't you worry about what it means." Her words were seasoned with her own brand of arrogance.

His eyebrows raised, but he said nothing.

"Just know that things are different now because I'm different."

He blew out an exaggerated breath. "Let me get something straight." A cold, icy smile slid across his face.

"This new Helen, this different Helen…" His voice trailed off as his eyes eased down her body. "Walks around half-naked, showing her nipples like she's in her twenties instead of dressing properly like a woman in her fifties?" He looked at her nipples, which poked through the thin fabric of her blue dress.

He cocked his head sideways. "Am I right…?!" His voice ratcheted up a notch.

With her arms akimbo, she just looked at him.

He saw a boldness in her stare that he'd never seen before. *She's downright insolent*, he thought.

He glared at her. "This Helen likes to talk to her husband like he's nobody? Is that it?! This different Helen doesn't want to cook for her husband or pick his clothes up at the cleaners, even though she's been doing it for years. Is that it?"

She said nothing.

"You're just going to stand there, looking at me, and not answer my question?" *You ungrateful bitch*, he thought, watching her.

She breathed in deeply but did not say a word.

"Since you seem bothered with me, I know a lot of women would trade places with you." He waved his hand around for emphasis. "Live in a house that's damn near a mini-mansion." Anger and gloating dripped from his words like sap from a tree.

Ever since we got married, I've worked my ass off, making a damn good living for this family. You and Ralph have never wanted for anything. I take care of everything.

She saw the pinched expression on his face, how his lungs rose and fell with each frustrated breath, and how his nostrils flared with his growing anger.

"I can't hear you. Cat got your tongue?" There was a harsh bitterness in his tone.

"How many of your friends would like to work only because they want to? Have a husband who takes care of them? Huh? Spend their money the way they want?!"

She exhaled. "Walt, I want to enjoy my Saturday doing exactly what I want, and it's not standing here listening to your macho bullshit. So, if you will excuse me, I'm going to get some coffee." She took several steps towards the kitchen.

"DON'T WALK AWAY FROM ME."

His loudness startled her. She turned and faced him and was greeted by a cold expression.

"You haven't answered even one of my questions." He enunciated every word as if it were necessary for her comprehension.

She crossed her arms, and like they had all the time in the world, she looked her fill at his body, from his bare feet to his tone legs and then up past his hips, flat stomach, and broad chest to his deliciously chocolate eyes.

"Walt, before I answer your questions, let me ask you something," she said around a soft chuckle. "I know you're into blue-moon sex…" She paused as his brow furrowed and he looked at her with a questioning scowl.

"What the fuck is blue-moon sex!?"

"That's when you like to have sex, every blue moon." Her smile mocked him as the truth of her words hit him like a bucket of ice water.

He glared at her. His temper was simmering hot, and if looks could kill, the police would've been called to report a crime.

He crossed his arms, silently fuming.

"Cat got your tongue?" She smirked and rolled her eyes. "Like I was saying, I know you're into blue-moon sex, but have you ever noticed that when we do have sex, I'm just saying the vowels with every stroke you make."

She mimicked a breathy tone she knew he would recognize. "*Aaaa, eeee, iiiii, oooo, uuuu.*"

He was so shocked at what she'd said, and without thinking, he drew back his hand and slapped her clean across her cheek. "YOU

UNGRATEFUL…" His voice trailed off as his anger got the best of him.

Her head swung to the right so quickly that she felt the jarring impact in her neck as it swiveled on its axis so hard that she felt dizzy. Burning, searing, and stinging needles of pain ripped through her like a thousand pinpricks.

Her hand instantly went to her cheek, trying to soothe it as gushing rivers of angry tears ran down her face.

Gurl, he don' slapped all da shit out yo tail. I told you nuthin' good was gon' come from pissin' off a man. You up here tellin' him you sayin' da vowels like he gon' be alright wit that. Umph, he 'bout as mad as a rattler.

Breathing deeply, she glared at him. Then she poked her finger in his chest as angry tears ran from her eyes. "MOTHERFUCKER, if you ever put your hands on me again, I'm going to tell Ralph to get two of his football friends to fuck you up! And I'll use my money to pay them!!"

She was ripping his ego to shreds, and he looked at her through narrow, angry eyes.

Fool, you's still standin' too close. You betta move back real slo like fo' he slaps da shit out you again, the old-lady voice cautioned.

She wasn't going to ignore the sage, old voice inside her head twice. She eased her foot back with a slowness that was barely noticeable.

"I SAID DON'T WALK AWAY FROM ME." Walt commanded.

Chapter 36

HE GLARED AT HER WITH A LOOK ON HIS face that resembled a person smelling rotten fish.

"First of all, don't you dare bring our son into this mess." His tone was firm as he raked his eyes down her body.

She looked at him, breathing deeply while tears ran from her eyes. Her cheek itched and burned like a lump of hot coal was taped to her face, and her neck throbbed with pain and was beginning to stiffen.

"And since you know how to recite the vowels, maybe you can learn how to say a few consonants. How about D, V, R, and C." His enunciation was clear and forceful. "If you add in the vowels, what does that spell? You ungrateful ass."

She knew her voice would wobble, so she didn't want to speak just yet. Instead, she wiped away her tears and steeled her spine, giving herself courage.

He was the father of her only child, the man she'd been married to for nearly thirty years, but with every ounce of her being, what she said next was perhaps the easiest thing she'd said all day.

She inhaled and slowly released her breath. "I tell you what…" She rubbed her aching neck. "Why don't you use those consonants yourself and start divorce proceedings. But hey, after I tell the judge that you hit me, I'm pretty sure I'll get whatever I want. And be sure that I'm going to tell every last one of your banking friends what you did."

He gasped, and his breath caught in his throat somewhere between his diaphragm and trachea.

She rolled her eyes. "Hell, you'll be lucky if you get to keep your job at the bank."

He wiped his hands down his face, feeling a sheen of cold perspiration as his father's words rang loud in his ears: *A man never hits a woman.* He'd drilled this into Walt's head as a young boy. *There's never an excuse, son.*

He took a deep breath. Desperate to stop the crisis they were in, he said with a placid voice, "I shouldn't have hit you." In the heat of the moment, he had lost his head and broken the first rule that his father had taught him.

There was a pained expression on his face at the realization of what he had done.

"Helen…I…um…" He waved his hands like he was waving a white flag. "Please…" He paused, trying to figure out what to say as his mouth went suddenly dry.

"Baby, I'm so sorry. I was angry and reacted without thinking, but there's no excuse for what I did. I was raised better than that."

Fresh tears pooled in her eyes, but at the moment, his apology did nothing to abate her anger.

"And when I talk to the judge, I'll tell him that I'm scared of you." She smirked. "Hell, when your golf buddies find out, they might not want to be associated with you."

He stumbled back onto the white settee and massaged his temples. The whole left side of his head throbbed like a fifty-pound weight was bearing down on the nerves.

"And all those women that you say would love to take my place, umph, I'm sure that number will dwindle to zero after they find out that you hit me."

She paused and looked him up and down. "I take that back. You might be able to find some desperate, ugly woman."

He hung his head. "Lennie, baby, I'm so very, very sorry. I had absolutely no right to hit you. I lost my temper."

He gazed at her, meeting her eyes. "But that was no call for my behavior, and I shouldn't have said some of those things. Baby, I'm so sorry. Will you please forgive me," he pleaded as his insides churned.

He let out a weary sigh. "Please, can you sit down and talk? I don't want to lose you. You're the only woman I have ever truly loved." His remorse was palpable. "Please. Let's talk. Please."

Barely able to look at her cheek, he swallowed the knot of guilt at the sight of the puffiness and redness. "Can you please find it in your heart to forgive me?" he said in a broken whisper.

As Helen watched the torment he was in, she felt an immediate and immeasurable sense of shame and guilt.

How can I not forgive him when I'm the one having an affair? She felt the sting of regret and exhaled slowly and sorrowfully. *Would he forgive me if he found out?*

Neither said anything while they watched and waited for the other to speak. He needed her to forgive him, and she needed to forgive him, knowing that she, too, would need his forgiveness.

I can't continue seeing Brenner and Irving. I can't go to Maui. I just can't. All I wanted was for things to be different and better between us.

How did we get here, Walt? She remembered how charming, sweet, sexy, and funny he could be.

She took a long, long breath and knew there was only one answer to his question. "Yes, Walt. I will forgive you." As soon as the words were out of her mouth, relief washed over his face.

They had ceased firing at one another.

"Thank you," he said quietly, "but I will make it up to you. I promise that I'm going to make things right between us."

He stood and walked towards her. "Can I hug you?" he asked with sadness in his voice.

She met his eyes, stepped into his embrace, and felt the warmth of his arms as they wrapped around her.

"I'm sorry, Lennie."

She remained quiet while thoughts of what she'd done haunted her. Allowing herself a respite, she just listened to his heartbeat.

"I'll make you an ice pack for your cheek and bring you two Tylenol and some water. Do you want to stay out here or go lie down?"

"You know, lying down sounds nice," she said as her head rested against his chest.

"Okay, I'll bring everything upstairs and put it on your nightstand."

He leaned his head down towards hers. "I'm going to say this a million times. I'm sorry," he whispered before kissing her hair.

Will you forgive me? she said in her mind, wondering if he would but fearing that he might not.

"I know you're hungry and probably have a headache," she said, lightening the mood. "I've already thawed some ground turkey, so I'll make you a turkey burger. That won't take long." She stepped out of his embrace and made her way towards the kitchen.

"No, I'll make me something. I want you to go lie down and get back to doing exactly what you want to do with your Saturday." There was a slight smile on his face.

"How about I just season the turkey for you and you do the rest?" she offered, partly from guilt and partly knowing that he wasn't a good cook.

He breathed in, still angry with himself for what he'd done. His shoulders slumped. "After what I just did, I would consider myself the luckiest man on the planet."

Chapter 37

AN UNLIT FIREPLACE WAS ON THE WALL directly in front of them. Lit hurricane candles burned while "Kiss of Life" by Sade played through his sound system.

Leelynn and Maxx were lying on the black velveteen chaise lounge in his front room.

His body was reclined while she straddled his lap. Her bent knees were snug against his thighs, and her arms were outstretched on either side of his shoulders as his head rested on the top of the chaise.

He picked up the last grilled shrimp from the platter he'd placed on a TV tray that he had positioned next to them.

"Open your mouth, baby."

"You've fed me so much already that I feel like I'm about to pop," she said softly while gazing at him.

He loved to cook and was great at it. "This is the last one." He patted her butt with his free hand. "Open up."

She leaned towards the perfectly seasoned crustacean that he held and slowly started licking wet circles around the shrimp and his fingers.

"Let's share it," she said. "Will you eat it, Maxx?" she purred as she nipped at the crustacean.

A wicked smile spread across his face at her double entendre. "Oh, I'm going to eat it, alright," he said in a smoky whisper as his hand massaged her lush buttocks.

"You promise," she said in a hushed tone as she licked the shrimp.

"I promise, baby." The heady sensations caused by her tongue made him growl low in his throat.

"Yesss," he said with a sigh as liquid heat seared through his body. *You have been in my dreams for a very long time*, he thought, easing his eyes over her beautiful face, framed by a head full of natural, soft curls.

She had dreamed of him nightly, and right now, she was on fire with the nearness of him. She loved that he had taken his locks down, letting them hang loose around his broad shoulders.

In fact, she loved everything about Maxx. His walk, his dark mocha eyes that seemed to sparkle whenever she was near. She loved his thoughts, his ideas, the color of his skin and the texture of his hair, which always seemed to smell of sandalwood.

She loved his body, muscular and ripped, loved the sentences that he spoke, the cadence of his voice, and the sound of his laughter. And she absolutely loved how he looked at her and wouldn't look away until he was ready.

She wasn't a desperate woman. Along with a successful photography business, she was beautiful, intelligent, and educated, and she had a wonderful family and great friends. She could have any man she wanted, but she had wanted Maxx from the moment she'd laid eyes on him.

She was thirsty for him and had no problem letting him know.

He was ruggedly handsome and had a bohemian swagger that reminded her of Lenny Kravitz. But his skin tone was darker and richer, like sun-roasted pecans. And there was instant chemistry between them, seductive yet real and meaningful, that neither could deny.

Ree had told her that he was in a relationship, and she had been, too. But as the fates would have it, those relationships would end, and there would be nothing standing in their way. This was their moment, their time.

She gazed into a pair of eyes that she'd seen up close countless times in her dreams. There were no ninety-day rules with him, only right-now rules, and whatever he wanted, she would give to him freely.

"That's my girl." A smile tugged at his lips as she bit into the shrimp.

His eyes never left hers. He popped the last bite in his mouth, and after swallowing, he pulled Leelynn closer, giving her another kiss on her already-kiss-swollen lips.

Holding his face in her hands, she sighed, "*Ahhh,*" feeling his tongue in her mouth. He was tasting her and lavishing her with his intimate taste.

Moments later, too soon for her liking, he ended the kiss and tugged on her hair.

"Let's go wash our hands and freshen up," he said. "And when we come back, I want you to take something off. And jewelry doesn't count." As he winked at her, he said to himself, *I'm falling in love with you.*

She smiled and glanced down at her bare feet. "What do you want me to take off?" Her voice was as soft as butter.

This was their moment, and Maxx and Leelynn intended to spend the weekend knowing that they would be together for all of time.

Chapter 38

"GOOD MORNING, HELEN," WALT SAID, walking into their bedroom with a heavily laden tray. "I was hoping you'd be up!"

"Good morning," she replied. "Yes, I'm up."

Like a lazy princess, she was still in bed. Fluffy white pillows were behind her back, propping her up. She intended to stay in today, read her book and magazines, and nurse the bruise on her cheek.

Yesterday, she'd taken Tylenol and kept a heating pad on her neck. Much of the stiffness was gone, and the ice pack that she'd kept on her face had removed the puffiness.

Their master suite was spacious and contemporary. A small chandelier hung from the ceiling. Although it might have seemed gaudy elsewhere, in their bedroom, it was perfect and added to the room's elegance. In the evenings, when it was turned on, prisms of light from its candle tubes danced across the room like a million stars.

They'd decorated the space in a beige that was so rich it would put you in mind of warm lattes. Pops of dark chocolate and celadon brought everything together beautifully.

The king-size bed was positioned against a back wall that faced the fireplace, which had a stone and glass-chip hearth.

A large floral abstract lithograph by Georgia O'Keefe hung above the mantel. Another floral abstract by the same artist was on the wall behind the couch in the sitting area, which was in an alcove just off from the fireplace.

As he approached, she tilted her head to the side and glanced at the clock on the nightstand. It was close to ten thirty.

"What do you have there?" she said pleasantly, meeting his eyes.

Still in her pink silk pajamas with black stitching around the lapel and down the front, she laid her book aside and smoothed out the comforter, at the same time pulling it up to her waist.

"My attempt at a Sunday brunch and an apology." He reached the side of the bed and placed the tray across her lap.

She smiled and looked down at the spread. Her eyes widened. "Wow!"

"I know I'm not a good cook, but I wanted to make you breakfast. I think it's edible." He chuckled a little, sliding his hands in his pockets. "I took my time, hoping to get everything right."

"Everything looks and smells wonderful!"

"Thank you." There was a boyish shyness in his tone.

He had prepared scrambled eggs with cracked pepper flakes, two strips of turkey bacon, and a slice of wheat toast. All were neatly arranged on the plate.

There was a bowl of watermelon chunks, and he had scooped out the seeds. A glass of fresh-squeezed orange juice was in a corner, and he'd rolled silverware in a white linen napkin.

"And you brought me flowers!" she teased, bringing the pink bloom to her nose.

He had broken off a sprig from the Framingham azalea bush in the backyard and placed it in a bud vase.

He chuckled. "That's the best I could do on such short notice. But don't worry. I'm going to do better."

"Very lovely!" She smiled as she put the vase back on the tray. "Thank you! This is wonderful! What are you up to today? More golf?" She picked up the linen napkin and unrolled the silverware.

"Yes, more golf. But I'm just going to work on my short game."

Her eyebrow rose, and she gave him an inquisitive look.

"Mainly chipping and putting," he provided.

"Got it! Well, as you can see, I'm not going anywhere further than this bed and the bathroom!"

He smiled. "I can tell! Enjoy your breakfast and I'm going to get going." He bent down and kissed her gently on her bruised cheek. It was still a deep blackish blue.

She got a good whiff of his cologne. "You smell nice!" she said, breathing in. The scent was masculine and exotic, yet surprisingly springtime, like the top note was rain.

After he ended the brief kiss, he cleared his throat. "I'm so sorry," he whispered before coming to stand at his full height. He caressed her cheek with the gentlest of strokes. He had tossed and turned in bed all night, kicking himself for hitting her.

"I'm sorry, too, Walt." She sighed. The taste of guilt coated her tongue as Brenner's and Irving's faces flashed in her mind.

Stop all that frettin', chile. Stop it! He jus feelin' guilty for slappin' da shit out of you. That's all. All's I wanna know is, will you get wit dem men agin? 'Cause I'm goin' set on the front row next time, bring me some pop-corn and wine! The old lady voice inside her head laughed.

Helen sighed as her eyes roamed over his handsome face. The light salt and pepper at his temples made him look distinguished. And when he wasn't dressed in golf shorts and a polo shirt like now, but in jeans or slacks and a shirt or his corporate attire, he looked debonair and sexy.

Meeting his eyes, she said in a near whisper, "Like I said yesterday, I accept your apology. While there's no excuse for what you did, I shouldn't have said those things to you." Like poking a giant sleeping bear with a big stick, she knew she had been goading him.

Neither looked away from the other as a rueful silence crept in; they were both trying to put Saturday behind them.

"Before I go, I'll set the alarm in case you doze off," he said, standing by the bed.

"Yes, please do that." She scooped up a forkful of eggs. "Umm! These are good." She gracefully covered her mouth as she talked.

He blew out a breath. "That's a relief."

His eyes lingered on her. Her hair was messy, but despite the bruise marring her caramel skin, she was absolutely beautiful. *There once was a time when you'd never let me see you without your hair combed. Something's going on with you. You're different, too different.*

"It's been a long time since I've seen your hair this messy," he said, reaching out to smooth down an unruly strand. There was amusement in his tone, but not an ounce of censure.

She smiled and looked up at him. "What's the use?" she said in a nonchalant tone. "I'm staying in bed all day."

"Nothing wrong with that." He chuckled.

She picked up the orange juice and took a healthy swallow. "This tastes so good! So sweet!" She set the glass back on the tray.

As he watched her, the look in his eyes suddenly changed.

"Let me taste. Please," he whispered as his eyes softened. He bent his head towards her again.

The timbre in his voice enveloped her as he lowered his mouth, easing his passion inside. His tongue slowly danced in her mouth, twirling lazily around hers, caressing its contours like fleeting wisps of butterfly wings.

As he kissed her, his thoughts ran rampant. *Why have you changed? What did you mean by 'a different path' and 'eye-opening'? You've never used profanity and acted the way you have lately. What's really going on with you?*

For the past several weeks, he'd been trying to reconcile the pieces of her that felt familiar with the pieces of her that felt new, different, and unrecognizable. *But I know who to call. Maybe she'll give me some answers.*

He slid a finger under her chin, bringing her mouth closer as he took an inordinate amount of time tonguing her.

A luscious tenderness took over, and she moaned softly in his mouth, "*Mmm.*"

He deepened the kiss. Being careful of the tray in her lap, she lifted her arms and wrapped them around his shoulders, greedily taking more.

She tasted the spearmint freshness in his mouth, while he tasted fresh-squeezed oranges.

She couldn't deny it; she loved the feel of his tongue. She feasted on his kiss as conflicting emotions nearly robbed the air in her lungs.

Moments later, he ended the kiss.

"I'll see you later," he said, brushing his finger across her bottom lip before giving her a soft peck on her bruised cheek.

As he straightened to his full height, he winked at her, and then he turned and made his way to the door.

She was speechless. Breathing slowly in and out, her eyes roamed freely down his backside as she watched his Denzel-like stride, one that she would know even in a dark, shadowy room.

He reached the threshold, and as he turned, smiled, and waved goodbye, his mind was racing and grappling for answers.

Chapter 39

THE MUSEUM WAS CLOSED ON MONDAYS, but Noel often came in. As the director, she used the quiet time to get things done that she couldn't manage during the week.

With her head buried in researching collections and exhibits, she barely heard her cell phone. But on the fourth ring, she quickly reached for it. She glanced at her watch. It was twenty minutes past ten.

"Walt?!" she said, closing the folder on her desk. "Good morning! How's it going?"

"I'm good. How are you? How's David?"

She leaned back in the leather chair and crossed her legs. "We're good! Still talking about the Fourth of July cookout at your house!"

"Did you guys have fun?"

"Of course! The cookouts get better and better every year. I've got to hand it to you. Your bar-b-que chicken is off the chain!"

"Thank you!" He loved grilling on his Weber Summit S-660 propane grill, and his and Helen's outdoor kitchen and beautifully landscaped backyard were worthy of a spread in *Architectural Digest* magazine.

She picked up her cup of coffee and groaned on the inside. She wasn't surprised by his call, knowing he might have sensed changes in Helen and would be curious about what was going on, but she sipped her morning java and pretended to be unaware.

"Actually, everything you grill is perfection! You know, we took a couple of plates home!" She chuckled. Leaning forward, she set the cup on a coaster.

"Don't you mean a couple of plates each?! Two for you and two for David?!" he teased good-naturedly.

"Like I said, we took a couple of plates home! That's simple math!" She laughed.

"Yeah, yeah! That's your kind of math! But hey, it's all good! Right?! Plus, it was a fun day!" Walt had gotten to know Noel and David, her husband, very well over the years, and he genuinely liked both of them.

"Speaking of food...umm... I was actually calling to invite you to dinner this evening. That is, if you're not busy."

"Invite me to dinner?" She feigned ignorance. "Shouldn't you be inviting your wife to dinner? Why me?" She chuckled.

"Well...umm." He let out a low, sheepish chuckle in his throat. "I was actually hoping to talk with you about my wife."

He needed answers, and who better to ask than her BFF, her ride-or-die chick, her bestie from way back?

"Talk to me about..." Her voice trailed off.

"I'm sorry for interrupting you, but I was hoping to get some information. You know, a little marital advice. You and David seem pretty happy."

Damn. She rolled her eyes. *Oh, Lord, here we go,* she groaned inwardly.

"What do you mean, give you a little information?" she said. "And remember, I'm a museum director, not a marriage counselor."

"Please, Noel," Walt implored. "I was really hoping to take you to dinner this evening. We could have a good time. I could feed your greedy ass and get a few answers at the same time. Kill two birds with one stone. That is, unless you've got a hot date with your hubby!" He held an anxious breath, needing her to say yes.

Walt knew the ladies confided in each other, and he knew without a doubt that Noel could answer any question he had, but he also knew she wouldn't betray Helen. He just hoped she'd give him enough tidbits and innuendos that he could string together.

"You can pick any restaurant. You name it!"

Walt was smart, and he'd pick apart her tone, or even the look on her face, for clues. Twist them together and fill in whatever holes he was trying to fill. *Dammit.* She sighed. *If you hadn't been such a butthole, you wouldn't need to ask me about your wife.*

"My marriage is in big trouble, and I know that you know that. Help a brotha out. You know my ass is in the damn dog house." There was genuine humility in his voice.

"I know that," she admitted.

"Oh! So, you know that? Please, Noel, let me take your greedy behind to dinner. I know you're not a marriage counselor, but I need your advice, and buying you dinner will be my way of paying for it."

"I tell you what," she said lightheartedly. "Sure! I'll let you treat me to dinner. And I charge by the half-hour for marital counseling!"

She would divulge nothing about Helen's affair. They'd become sisters, and there was a deep line in the sand that she'd never cross, and that included sharing the contents of any of their conversations.

"Thank you." He sighed with relief. "How about I get my assistant to make reservations at Henry's for six? Unless you want to go someplace else."

"Nope, Henry's is fine, and six, it is." She leaned forward, picked up her pen, quickly jotted down the time on a Post-it, and stuck it on the open page in her slim daytimer calendar.

"Great! I really appreciate it!"

"Oh! Before I forget, Devon is getting married!" she said playfully. Swiveling in her chair, she turned to face the floor-to-ceiling windows.

"Wow!" He chuckled. "I like Devon. So, he finally popped the big question?!"

"Yes, he did!" She brushed a piece of lint from her ripped boyfriend jeans. She'd rolled them at the ankle and paired them with a black cotton shirt tied at her waist. A pair of black mesh slide mules with tiny lemon-drop pom-poms in the center completed her look.

"Devon's cool. Killer on the golf course!" He paused to take a sip of his coffee. "Tell him I said congrats!"

"I will. We're so excited! David's going to be the best man. And of course, you and Helen are invited to the wedding. It's going to be in March, but they haven't set the date yet!"

"I'm happy for them."

"Me, too!" You could hear the excitement she felt for her brother-in-law. "The ceremony will be at a little chapel in Pittsboro," she said before taking another sip of her now-tepid coffee.

"That's great. Just let us know the date."

"Will do!" She smiled.

She heard him take a deep breath and then clear his throat.

"I know we're getting together for dinner, but can I ask you something now?" he said, glancing at the silver-framed photo of Helen on his credenza.

He massaged his temple, hoping to relieve the tension that had rooted there, and tried to find the courage to ask what he dreaded most.

"Sure." Her perfectly arched eyebrows scrunched up at the change in his voice. Gone was his cheery tone, replaced now by a more subdued one.

He took a deep, settling breath. "Is my wife having an affair?"

Chapter 40

IT WAS SIX THAT EVENING.

White wispy clouds drifted on a slow current in the sky, and a light wind flirted with the leaves on the trees. The sweet fragrance of honeysuckle wafted through the air like misty puffs from a perfume atomizer.

Walt had to drive two blocks over from Henry's to Maple Lane to find a parking space. He glanced in his rearview mirror. Seeing no cars behind him, he pulled alongside the green Honda Accord and slowed to a stop.

"Driftin' on a memory. Ain't no place I'd rather be, than with you, yeah…" he sang with the Isley Brothers as he put the car in reverse. He eased the tail end of his late-model black Lexus into the open space between the Honda and a 960 Volvo.

"I wanna be livin', for the love of you…" he maneuvered the back end of his car in position before straightening the wheel. Then he inched the car forward, glancing in the rearview mirror to check the distance. Finally, he put the Lexus in park and turned off the engine.

As he unfastened his seatbelt, he glanced at the clock on the car's console.

"I better text Noel. Let her know I just parked," he said as he unbuttoned the top three buttons on his light blue dress shirt.

"Lovely as a ray of sun…" he sang. Using his index finger, he typed:

Just parked b there in 10 mins W.

He sent the text and slipped the phone in his front shirt pocket.

"I wanna be livin', for the love of you…" He adjusted his dark sunglasses on the bridge of his nose, unlocked the door, and got out. Holding the key fob over his shoulder, he pressed lock.

He slid the fob in his pocket, and as he made his way up the street, he unbuttoned his shirt cuffs. His necktie and navy-blue suit jacket were already hanging from a wooden hanger in the backseat.

Maple Lane was one of the prettiest streets in downtown St. Winter. On both sides stood red maple trees that had been planted years ago. At this time of year, the foliage on the trees was an array of burgundy red leaves mixed with the rich, dark green of older leaves.

Light brown "whirlers," or "whirligigs," spiraled through the air like helicopter blades. The samaras landed everywhere, on tops of hoods and trunks, and one landed in his outstretched hand.

He smiled and slipped it in his shirt pocket, hoping it would bring him good luck.

As he made his way up the street, he thought about Helen. Deep down he had little expectations that he'd get any useful information from Noel; after all, the ladies were as thick as thieves, and he'd be lucky if she threw him a short bone.

Chapter 41

AS WALT REACHED THE SIDEWALK, AN elderly couple came up behind him.

"It's nice out, isn't it?" He smiled and glanced over his shoulder. Considerate of their pace, he slowed his long stride, allowing them to catch up.

"Sure is," the old man said with a pleasant nod. His bald head, mostly covered under a linen hound's tooth cap, glistened with a sheen of perspiration. He was wearing a pair of light khaki pants and a beige guayabera.

The elderly woman, whose arm was tucked gently in the crook of her husband's elbow, had on a pair of white fitted capri slacks and a blush-colored short-sleeve knit top.

"How are you, ma'am?"

"I'm fine, young man," She smiled with a regal, penetrating glint in her eyes as she looked at him.

The melodious richness in her voice was surprising. It was lush, smooth like mink. And her words were enunciated with a crispness; it was obvious she was an educated and well-traveled soul.

Was she an opera singer? Walt wondered, but he did not ask as he gazed at the elderly couple, easily seeing a treasure trove of love between them.

Walt thought about his relationship with Helen. *Will we be fortunate enough to be walking together in our eighties?* he asked himself, assuming the couple's age.

He glanced at the pair and smiled. "If you don't mind me asking, what is the secret to your happy marriage?" *This is a rare opportunity,* he thought, realizing that, other than his folks, he didn't know too many elderly couples he could ask this question. *I can't let this moment slip by.*

"It's obvious that you two have something special and unique." He briefly met the woman's eyes before looking back at the older man.

"Are you asking me or my husband?" the elderly woman asked.

He chuckled at the feather-soft censure in her tone. "I'm asking you, ma'am."

With the graceful, fluid movements of a ballerina, she lifted her free hand and caressed the floral pink silk scarf draped around her neck as if soothed by its touch.

"Our secret, young man, is that, we, in all things, in all ways, and always, make love."

Walt drew in a surprised breath. Never in a million years had he expected this serene-looking matron to utter the words "make love."

As she glanced his way, the woman's eyes sparkled, and her smile captivated him. Then she looked away.

"I can tell by the look on your face that you were not expecting me to say something as provocative as that." She chuckled low in her throat. "But I did say it." A hint of sassiness peppered her tone. "And if you do not suffer from a prosaic mind, you'll know that making love is more than a sexual act. It is also walking with your partner…"

Her voice trailed off as she gazed lovingly at her husband. "Feeling the warmth of his hand in yours."

Breathing in gently, she glanced down. "Take this scarf..." She held the silk ends between her fingers and caressed it. "I remember the day my husband wrapped this wonderful, unexpected gift around my neck. When he tied it, he kissed me sweetly on my lips."

She gave her husband a smile before continuing. "You see, tender moments like these and so many more are simply moments to..." She looked at Walt expectantly.

"Make love," he murmured.

The older man tapped him on the forearm, getting his attention.

"And know this, young man. Your actions, tokens given as an apology resulting from a spat, are not the same," the man said with a wisdom that Walt listened intently to. "Because the genesis of that comes from a place of reparation, and that's never a good place to be, at least not in a marriage."

Chapter 42

AS THEY MADE THEIR WAY DOWN THE
sidewalk, they walked under the low-hanging cluster of tree branches
that draped over like a natural canopy. The foliage shaded and cooled
the spot with its expanse of greenery.

That's when the advice from the elderly couple landed on him like
a bucket of cold water, and without thought, Walt slid his hand in his
pocket until he felt the dime that he knew would be there.

"Dammit," he said sotto voce.

He was unaware that the elderly couple glanced at him. Seeing that
he was consumed, they shared a knowing gaze and contented themselves with the enjoyment of their evening stroll while he rummaged
through his past mistakes.

Walt exhaled as ugly realities formed in his head and his mind
started drifting. As clear as day, he could see Helen's face from the night
she'd tried to seduce him. *She was so sweet and sensual, and I pushed her
away.*

He thought about his reaction to her boudoir photos and remembered how she had cooked him his favorite meal of meatloaf and green

beans. *I acted like a damn fool rather than tell her the truth, that she looked sexy as hell in every photo. Sexier than those women on my phone, that's for damn sure. But like a fucking asshole, I made her think that I didn't approve.*

And when was the last time, other than for her birthdays, Mother's Day, and Christmas, that I gave her a gift? He exhaled, growing angrier with himself. *I used to buy her gifts all the time. Do little things for her that I knew she liked.*

The cumulation of his mistakes began to settle on his shoulders like wet sandbags, and he breathed deeply and rubbed his hand down his face.

I've taken my wife for granted, plain as day. I've provided for her and for Ralph, for sure. Financially. I let that be enough. Got comfortable with that. Stood on my money like a king on a damn throne. I stopped courting Lennie a long time ago. Stopped providing the tenderness that she needed and wanted, that our marriage needed. I stopped making her feel special and stopped making memorable moments.

He sighed at the gravity of his actions. *We've just become a married couple in a big house together. And if that wasn't bad enough, I yelled at her and slapped her so hard that it left a nasty bruise.*

Walt exhaled loudly.

Noticing that Henry's was the next stop, he slowed his steps. "Please accept my apology," he said.

An embarrassed smile was on his face as he glanced at the restaurant's entrance. A thick, ropey vine of bougainvillea arched over the doorway like a headband made of velvety petals. Pink blooms lay scattered along the sidewalk like an aisle for a bride.

"I seemed to have forgotten my manners. My mind wandered, and I just stopped talking," he said, realizing that he'd become absorbed in his own thoughts and hadn't said a word the last couple of minutes.

"Not a problem at all, young man," the elderly man said. "Walking has a way of helping clear the mind."

Walt wished he had more time to talk, knowing that anything this couple said would be profound.

"Yes, it does, and what you all said made me think about a lot of things. This is my stop. I'm meeting someone here for dinner. I'm Walt, by the way. Walt Gothrock." He extended his hand in greeting.

As he shook the elderly man's hand, he was struck by the strength of the man's grip.

"Well, Mr. Gothrock, I'm Dr. Bill Bennett. We're pleased to make your acquaintance," the man said with a slight incline of his head as he shook Walt's hand. "And this beauty standing next to me..." He paused, slightly turning his head. "Is the lovely Mrs. Macheria Bennett." His voice was filled with adoration.

Walt freed his hand and reached for her delicate-looking hand.

She had been watching him. The expression on her face was warm and motherly yet mysterious.

"Mrs. Bennett." He smiled as he wrapped his larger hand around hers. "It has been my absolute honor to meet you and Dr. Bennett today."

He glanced at her husband briefly before returning his attention to her.

"Thank you, Mr. Walt Gothrock. It has been an honor meeting you as well," she said in a voice that was as rich and full as her refined beauty.

"Thank you, ma'am." Walt bowed his head in a courtly gesture as he eased his hand away.

Reaching into his back pocket, he pulled out his wallet, from which he retrieved two business cards. He closed it and slid the dark brown billfold back. He gave one card to Mrs. Bennett and the other to Dr. Bennett.

They glanced down briefly to read the information and then looked up again.

Walt gently laid his hand on her shoulder with the lightest of touches. "Ma'am, I will never forget the advice that you gave me." He met her eyes, which seemed to be looking inside of him.

"I know you will not," she said.

Walt smiled, feeling a bit of the weight had lifted, and eased his hand from her shoulder. "And Dr. Bennett, I will not forget your advice, either. Both of you have given me so much. I cannot thank you enough. And if you ever need anything…" He tapped his business card in the man's hand. "Please do not hesitate to reach out to me. I mean this sincerely."

"Thank you. We might just pop up one day." The older man chuckled. "Stop in to say hello."

"Anytime. I'll drop whatever I'm doing to visit with you!" Walt said, hoping that he and Helen might one day get to know this couple. "Do you have any more advice that you can spare a man who's been a fool?"

The older man smiled and tapped Walt's arm. "Yes, I do, young man. Life is a collection of trillions of moments, and only the dim-witted fritter them away, devalue them, or squander them. Remember, make every moment count, for you'll never get that twinkle of time back. Do you understand," he said in a fatherly tone.

Walt smiled. "Yes, sir, I do. And again, thank you both for the advice." He bowed his head slightly.

"Very well, enjoy your dinner, and this lovely woman and I shall be on our way."

Walt looked from one to the other, knowing that he'd never forget them. "I wish you continued health and Godspeed," he said before they resumed their evening stroll.

Mrs. Macheria Bennett glanced back at him over her shoulder; she winked and waved goodbye as her floral pink silk scarf lifted and fluttered in the gentle breeze.

Walt smiled. Determined not to let this moment slip by, he blew her a sweet kiss.

And when her eyes lit up with a smile, Walt hoped that he and Helen would be lucky enough to stroll hand in hand down the sidewalks in St. Winter until they were old and gray.

Chapter 43

"EVENING, SIR. WELCOME TO HENRY'S."
The hostess's voice was cheerful.

Walt smiled. "Good evening, miss."

"Do you have a reservation with us?"

"Yes, I do. It's under Gothrock," he said before looking down at his watch. "I'm a few minutes late."

"No worries! Let me check." The young woman scrolled through the computer reservation log.

While she did that, he glanced around the restaurant. Many tables were filled with folks enjoying their evening. "Sinnerman," sung by Nina Simone, played through the speakers while laughter and conversations permeated the air.

"Great. I see it right here. Your party has already arrived. Come with me."

"That won't be necessary. I'll save you the steps. She's right over there." He pointed in Noel's direction.

She was seated at a corner table by the window. She was glancing down at her cell phone, but he'd know her sandy-reddish hair anywhere.

"Well, then, enjoy your meal!"

"Oh, I'm sure I will! Thank you!" He headed towards their table.

Mouthwatering aromas of sizzling meats, grilled onions and vegetables, and spices mingled and fused into a heady and intoxicating scent that made his stomach growl.

She looked up, their eyes met, and they shared a smile as she waved.

"He's here. I'll talk with you later. Love you." She disconnected her call and laid the phone on the table.

From this vantage point, she had an unobstructed view, and without meaning to, she eased her eyes down Walt's body—not in a sexual way, but hell, she wasn't blind, either. *He's good looking. I've got to give it to him,* she thought.

Walt was at least six feet tall. His skin was the color of milk chocolate, and he had a walk that drew women's attention like bees to honey. It was masculine and confident yet smooth and relaxed, like he had a million dollars in his back pocket.

As he reached the table, she looked up at him and said, "Helen said to tell you hello!"

His eyes widened, and she laughed at his crestfallen look.

"Dammit, Noel! I asked you not to tell her we were having dinner," he said, leaning down and planting a kiss on her cheek.

As he bent over her, she smelled his cologne and breathed in his summertime scent. *Perfect for the warm weather*, she thought.

He came around to his side of the table, pushed back the chair, and took a seat.

"Just for that, I'm not buying your ass dessert. And I'm not going to tell you that you look nice, even though you do," he said in a tone that feigned annoyance.

He squinted his eyes. "What did my lovely wife have to say?" He paused and looked around for the waiter. "Hit me upside the head with a plate of food."

The memory was still fresh in his mind of Helen doing just that.

She chuckled. "That was David on the phone!"

He breathed a sigh of relief. "Oh, you got jokes?!"

He looked at her; he'd always thought the penny-brown freckles on the bridge of her nose gave her a perpetually youthful look. "So, you haven't said anything to her?"

"Not yet." Noel smiled. "And tell me this, Walt. Why would Helen tell me to hit you upside the head?" She glared at him.

He broke their eye contact and glanced around. "Before you start interrogating my ass…" He wiped his hand down his face. "I need a drink! Where's our waiter?" He looked over one shoulder and then the other.

Though he and Noel had become friends over the years, he knew that he'd have to tread lightly this evening. He didn't want to say the wrong thing or too much.

Finally, he made eye contact with a waiter.

The young man nodded in acknowledgment, and Walt turned back around to face Noel, who was glaring at him impatiently.

With his elbows on the table, he steepled his fingers in front of his mouth and rested his chin on top of his thumbs. "How are things at the museum?"

She playfully rolled her eyes, disregarding what he'd asked. "You haven't answered my question, Walt. Why would Helen tell me to hit you upside the head?" She gave him a sassy yet playful attitude as she crossed her arms. "I'm waiting."

"I told you I need a drink first, Annalise Keating." He chuckled at his wife's free-spirited friend. *I see Helen's picking up some of your fashion ways*, he said to himself.

"Yeah, yeah, Viola Davis in *How to Get Away with Murder* wouldn't take pity on you by letting you drink first."

"You're right." He took a deep breath. "But I'm saved by the waiter!" He glanced up as the young man arrived at their table.

"Alright! I'll give you a reprieve!" She smiled.

"Good evening. Welcome to Henry's. I apologize for your wait," the waiter said, setting two glasses of water on the table before sliding free the two menus wedged under his arm.

He handed one to Noel and then to Walt.

"I'll give you a moment to look over the dinner menu, but perhaps I can interest you in something to drink first."

"Yes, you may!" Walt said with an emphatic tone, and he gestured at Noel. "Ladies first."

"I'll have a French 75," she said, meeting the waiter's eyes.

"Excellent choice, madame." The waiter smiled and turned to Walt. "And for you, sir?"

"Let me get an old fashioned, heavy, on the rocks."

"Another excellent choice! I'll put these orders in. Take your time looking at the menus." The waiter stepped away.

Walt said, "While we're waiting for our drinks, let me ask you a question."

"Oh, so you can't answer my question, but you can ask me one? Things at the museum are fine!" she teased.

"Work with a brotha, Noel!" He paused. Judging from the look in her eyes, he knew he had a slim window. "Just a simple question for now." His fingers beat a nervous rhythm on the table.

"Okay, one!" she said, cocking her head to the side like a diva.

He took a deep breath. "Did Lennie say anything to you about those boudoir pictures that she took? Specifically about me. You know. My reaction?"

She leaned across the table and got in his face. "Of course she told me. I know all about it. And just for the record, you pissed her off to the highest degree of pisstivity. You basically shut her down like she was some child who needed scolding."

Her tone was subdued, but her bite was clear.

It was tough hearing the truth, and it left a pregnant pause hanging in the air as neither said anything for a moment.

He exhaled his frustration. "Yeah, I know. I fucked up. If I could take back that day, I would a million times over."

She could see the worried lines crease his forehead.

He was so confident and sure of himself that it had to hurt to eat a slice of humble pie by asking her for marital advice. She felt a little sorry for him, but knowing about Helen's affair, she also knew his timing was a day late and a dollar short.

"Here you go!" the waiter said as he approached their table.

"Alright!" Walt said, ready for the spirits to relax him.

"One French 75 for the lady." The young man placed her drink on the table.

"Thank you. This looks great," Noel said, looking at the slender champagne flute. A long, curled ribbon of lemon hung from the rim of the glass, and bubbles popped and fizzled inside the crystal glass.

"I hope you enjoy it!" He smiled at her. "And for you, sir, an old fashioned, heavy, on the rocks." The waiter set the drink on the table in front of Walt. "I hope it's to your satisfaction."

"Well, let's see!" Walt picked up the drink and took a generous sip.

The Kentucky whiskey, bitters, and muddled sugar heated a smooth trail down his throat, setting little fires along the way as it licked a path to his stomach.

He sighed and gave the waiter an appreciative smile. "This is perfect!" He set the glass down. "Compliments to the bartender." He gave him a thumbs-up.

"That's what we like to hear!" The young man smiled. "Are you ready to order dinner, or shall I give you more time?"

Noel glanced at Walt, giving him the mean eye. "He's been talking my ear off. We haven't even looked at the menu. Even though I know what I want, I don't think he does." She chuckled before taking a sip of her drink.

"Guilty as charged," he said, tilting his head sideways. "Can you give us a few more minutes?" He looked up at the waiter.

"Absolutely. Take your time. I'll check on you two in a few minutes."

Walt reached for the stirrer and swirled it around in the drink. The crisp clinking of ice cubes against the side of the glass sounded like tubular bells.

"So..." He paused, leaned forward, and picked up his glass, ready to propose a toast.

"What are we toasting?!" Noel's eyes widened as she lifted her own glass. She could see the wheels in his head turning.

"We're toasting me," He took a deep breath.

She gave him a curious look.

"Here's to me." He clinked her glass. "For being the biggest fool and asshole for messing things up with my gorgeous wife."

Walt's self-deprecating tone was evidence that he'd finally admitted to himself that his marriage had been slowly slipping through his fingers, bit by bit, like grains of sand.

Chapter 44

"AND THAT, MY DEAR FRIEND, IS THE truth!" Noel laughed before taking a sip of her champagne cocktail.

"What can I say? When I mess up, I do it big time!" Walt brought the lowball to his lips and took a generous swallow.

"Ooh, that's good!" He took another sip while his mind raced. His instincts were telling him what he didn't want to believe. *But I've got a bad feeling, 'cause something doesn't feel right. She's too different.*

He sat forward and rested his forearm on the table. "Before our waiter comes back, let me ask you again. It's one of the most important questions that I have." He sighed and eased back in his seat, his eyes never leaving hers.

"Walt, you know your wife and I are best friends, and I take our relationship very seriously. So, brotha, I hope you don't think I'm going to sit here and betray my friendship with her."

"I suspected you would say that." He chuckled. "But I'm going to ask you again anyway." He held his glass and rotated his wrist, round and round, swirling the whiskey.

He took a deep breath. "Is my wife having an affair?"

"I know things are bad between you two, but if you want to know the answer to that question, you should talk to Helen. Not me."

Walt smiled, but it didn't reach his eyes. He set his glass down and reached for her hand, and when she placed her hand in his, he laced his fingers through hers.

"You know…" He sighed as he looked down at their joined hands. "That's exactly the answer I was dreading you'd give. Because if Helen wasn't having an affair…" He looked up at her with sadness in his eyes. "I'd expect you to say something like, 'Walt, you know Helen wouldn't do something like that. She loves you.'"

"Don't go playing Johnny Cochran on me!" She gave him a chuckle, trying to redirect his thoughts. "But seriously, since I'm supposed to be giving you marital advice, let me just say communication is key. K-E-Y." She slowly said each letter. "Talk to Helen. Ask her."

"Thanks, Oprah," Walt teased.

The waiter came over and said with a smile, "It looks like you all are deep in conversation, but have you had a chance to look at the menus, or should I come back? It's no rush."

Walt and Noel looked up, and with a sheepish grin, he unlaced their fingers. "Don't blame her. It's my fault. As soon as you left, I started asking her questions."

"Walt, everything here is good, so you can't go wrong." She smiled, picked up her menu, and gave it back to the waiter. "I already know what I want."

"Okay. You go ahead and place your order while I look at the menu." He glanced at the wide selection.

"I'll have the salmon and lamb tapas with white rice and that fabulous pomegranate and pineapple dipping sauce." She wiggled in her seat, excited about her meal.

"That's one of my favorites," the young man said, scribbling her order on a tiny sheet of paper.

"Walt, Helen had this the last time we were here and loved it!"

"Well, that's settled." He closed the menu and handed it to the waiter. "If my wife loved it, I'm sure I will."

The waiter acknowledged his order with a nod.

"How do you like your lamb cooked, madam?"

"Well done, but not dry."

"Got it!" the waiter said, turning towards Walt.

"And for you, sir?"

"Same for me." Walt watched the waiter jot down their preferences. "Oh, um…let me get one of these dinners to go. I'll take it home to my wife."

"Walt, that's so nice of you. I'll do the same for David! And please put everything on his tab!" She chuckled and pointed at Walt.

"Certainly, madam!" The waiter smiled. "I'll get these orders in. Would either of you like another drink?"

"Yes! Another French 75!" Noel giggled. "Just make sure you put all of this on his tab!" She gestured animatedly with her hand before taking another sip of her cocktail.

"But of course!" The young man was enjoying the friendly banter.

Walt just shook his head in mock disgust. "When my dinner comes, I'll have another old fashioned, heavy, on the rocks. Dealing with this one, I've got to stay on my toes." He nodded in Noel's direction.

"I completely understand, and I'll be sure to put everything on your tab!" The waiter laughed before turning to leave.

"Well, since I'm buying you and your husband's dinner, you have to give me some answers, Noel. Come on. You got to help me out."

He took a generous sip of his drink. The ice cubes had melted some, slightly watering down his drink.

"Look, I'm not throwing my girl under the bus no day of the week. Come on. You know this. Just talk to her, Walt."

Noel picked up her glass. "But since you're paying for everything, I will tell you this…" She took a sip. "This tastes so good!" She set the flute on the table and leaned towards him like she had a secret.

Walt was listening.

"Helen is sick and tired of you not paying her any attention, and she was hurt by you having photos of those women on your phone!"

"They're off, okay?" He waved his hand in disgust. "Every last one! Gone! But I need you to tell me something that I don't know." Walt adjusted his seat. "Let me ask you this. Speaking of photos, what's the name of the photographer who took her boudoir pictures?"

"Why?! Are you going to take her to court, try to close her business?!" she teased.

"Noel, just give me the damn name," he said, pretending to be annoyed. "And no, I'm not going to do either." He playfully rolled his eyes. "What's her name, Lee something?"

When Noel didn't say anything for a moment, he said, "Just tell me. Please. Helen has hidden her photo album from me, and I want to get another." He slid his hand up and down the lowball. The icy condensation wet his fingers.

She sighed. "Alright. Her name is Leelynn Floyd, and her studio is in Charlotte. Actually, I have a photo shoot myself. And I'll tell you one thing…" She wagged her finger. "If David acts like an asshole like you did when I show him my photos, you better add another room to that doghouse you're living in because he will be joining you."

She cocked her head to the side and rolled her eyes, driving her point home.

Walt threw his head back and laughed. "Hell, I'm calling David and telling him to drool out the side of his mouth when you show him your photos. Tell him to start shaking and shit!" Walt shook his arms wildly like he was trembling.

"Shut up!" She leaned across the table and hit him.

"You think I'm joking." He laughed. "I'm callin' his ass and givin' him a clue. Save him some misery."

Walt reached for his cell phone. "Pardon me one second." *Please pick up*, he pleaded silently as he dialed Helen's number. *Please.*

Noel leaned back in her chair, picked up her drink, and took a generous sip.

He breathed a sigh of relief when she answered on the third ring.

"Hey. How are you feeling?" His voice was low and smooth. "That's good. Listen, I'm having dinner with a friend and wanted to let you know that I'd be late…" He paused as she responded.

"I'm at Henry's, so I'll bring you the lamb and salmon tapas and some of the pomegranate sauce, okay? I'll see you in a couple of hours. I love you, Helen."

Walt ended the call and laid his phone on the table. He was desperate to get things right with his wife, and he intended not to waste any time getting started.

"Well, well, look at you. I'm impressed. Sounding all sexy." Noel smiled.

"I heard you, Noel. Thank—"

"Walt, let me say this…" Noel paused. "And sorry for interrupting you."

"I'm all ears." He took a sip of his old fashioned.

"Your window is closing fast, so don't let the cement dry before you fix things with Helen, because soon it will be too late. Do you understand?"

"I understand." Walt slowly nodded. The expression on his face revealed his comprehension of just how bad things were.

His instincts kept telling him that Helen was having an affair, but the advice from the Bennetts replayed in his head like a broken record, and he'd live by those words until his instincts gave him proof.

Chapter 45

THE SHADOW OF THE BRUISE WAS GONE, but Helen eased closer to the vanity mirror to be sure.

"Nothing," she said and brushed her fingers over the once-tender spot.

She'd called in sick yesterday, Monday, and spent the time nursing the bruise on her cheek and getting rid of the stiffness in her neck.

But today she was A-okay. Making her way down the hall, she stopped in her office to grab her briefcase and purse before taking the stairs leading to the kitchen.

"Good morning!" Walt's eyes lit up as soon as he saw her. "You look fantastic!"

She was wearing a deep purple skirt with a peplum bottom trimmed in white topstitching, a white short-sleeve knit shell, and a black leather belt. On her feet were a pair of snakeskin slingbacks. Diamond studs with dangling turquoise teardrops sparkled from her earlobes.

He was leaning against the granite countertop, scrolling through his emails on his cell phone, but he laid his phone down and, with outstretched arms, walked over to her.

With a look of mild surprise in her eyes, she stepped into his embrace.

They'd pushed the fiasco of last Saturday to the back of their minds; he had pushed the warning from his instincts back there as well.

"Hi there!" he said softly as he wrapped his arms around her waist and rubbed his chin across the top of her head.

"Good morning. You're not going into the bank today? Where are the dark pants and white shirt?" she said with hints of sarcasm.

"Haha, yes, I'm going into the office today. You're not the only one changing up your wardrobe!" He kissed her forehead and stepped back. "Since you've started dressing differently, I thought I better get on board." He chuckled and turned in circles like a model.

He had on a pair of dark taupe slacks and a crisp black shirt, sans a necktie. On his waist was a dark brown and black two-toned leather belt with a simple gold buckle. A pair of black calf-leather penny loafers were on his feet.

She smiled. "I see. Don't be surprised if folks look at you like you're crazy. I haven't seen you in a black dress shirt in a hundred years." She dropped her things on the counter by the butler's door.

"Well, do you like how I look?" He put his hands in his pockets and struck a pose.

"I do!" As she walked towards the coffee pot, her gaze eased up and down his body. "You look really nice." She met his eyes. *What's up with the 180? You're beginning to act more like the Walt I fell in love with.*

"Thanks. I made breakfast this morning. And yes, it's edible!"

Fresh-brewed coffee was on the counter, and a small plate with buttered toast and crispy strips of turkey bacon sat on the stove.

"You got time to eat, or do you want me to put your food on a paper towel so you can take it with you?"

"I've got time." She glanced at her watch. "I was going to stop at McDonald's, but what you prepared is fine." She filled a cup with coffee and cream, stirred it, and set the cup on the table before making her way to the stove, where she picked up the small plate.

His eyes followed her every move and every luscious curve on her body, which was enticingly displayed by her outfit.

"You look fantastic!" he said, leaning against the counter.

"You said that already." She chuckled and sat at the kitchen table.

"Yeah, I did, didn't I?" He gave her a sexy wink, cocked his head to the side, and pointed to what she was wearing. "I know I haven't said it, but I really do like the things you've been wearing lately. All very pretty!" He walked to the table, sat down, and slid his chair closer to hers.

He took a sip of his coffee and gazed at her. "I know it was a minute before I caught up to liking your new clothes, but I'm here now."

Her eyebrow scrunched up in mocked confusion. "Who's this imposter sitting next to me?! And what have you done with my husband?" she teased before taking a bite of turkey bacon.

Walt threw his head back in a fit of laughter, and his chocolate eyes warmed with humor.

When he stopped laughing, he brushed his finger across her bottom lip. "I haven't told you how beautiful you are lately, have I?"

"Oh!" She waved her hands in the air. "Now I know you're an imposter!" She laughed. "Complimenting me on my outfit. Telling me I'm beautiful? Who are you?!!" She raised her eyebrows. "You better talk fast, mister, before I file a missing person report!!"

A part of her wept on the inside for what she'd done, but in a polar-opposite way, her affair had filled the other half of her with a rapture that was undeniable. And oddly, she had been left with a sense of freedom to do whatever she wanted, knowing that her life was meant to be lived and enjoyed.

She looked at him. "I get it. You're just feeling guilty. That's why you're being so nice." She wiped her hands on the napkin.

"Yes," he whispered, "I will always feel guilty for hitting you, and I promise you, Lennie, I'll never, ever hit you again." There was a vulnerability in his voice. "And let's just say I've had a conversation with three little birdies that told me I better get my shit together," he added as he gently stroked her arm.

"Three little birdies?" She smiled. "So, Dr. Dolittle, you talk to birds now?!" She wiggled her eyes with levity as she bit into a slice of toast.

"Yes! I'm talking to birds and anything else that will give me advice. And no, my dear wife…" He tilted her chin up with his middle finger and nudged her face towards his. "I'm not an imposter. I'm just a man who realizes what a fool he's been," he said softly before leaning in closer.

"And the reason I'm being so nice is because I want to be. I want things good between us again." He took a deep breath. "You deserve nothing less, and the real reason I said you are beautiful is because you are." He eased her onto his lap, wrapped his arm around her waist, and trailed his other hand up and down her back.

"Wow!" she murmured at this unexpected romantic moment. *Oh my God, he smells so good.* Bringing her nose just below the dip between his neck and collarbone, she breathed him into her lungs and sighed as the warmth of his hands soothed her like a balm.

His scent left her desperate to taste him, and as if her life depended on it, she stuck out her tongue and licked him like a cat.

Walt let out a groan, low and soft, like a guttural whisper. He was no longer caught off guard by her wanton behavior. In fact, it turned him on.

"Yes, good morning, my beautiful wife," he whispered in a sultry tone.

When their eyes met, he took possession of her mouth in a most sensual way.

Helen was late for work because she stayed on Walt's lap for another hour while he fed her toast, turkey bacon, coffee, and lots of sweet morning kisses.

Chapter 46

"IRVING, THANK YOU FOR DRIVING OUT here today and on such short notice," Dr. Linda Dalcoe said.

She was the headmistress at the A. Pearl Academy, where he had served as board chair for the past five years. The students were gone for the summer, but administrators and staff often worked part time throughout the summer months.

The charter school was within the flight path of the Charlotte Douglas International Airport and was for boys grades four to twelve. The school focused on comprehensive language arts, science, technology, and math and had a thematic approach that incorporated aeronautics.

"No worries. Besides, I wouldn't have been able to concentrate the whole day without knowing what was in this letter." He sat in the upholstered chair in front of her large wooden desk. "I know you're loving the peace and quiet with the little kiddies gone!"

She smiled. "Don't tell anybody, but yes, I am!" She chuckled. "In a way, it's the best time of the year for me."

He laughed. "Your secret is safe with me." His hazel eyes sparkled in the ribbons of sunshine streaming through her office windows. "Tell me about this sealed envelope that you received with my name on it."

She had called him as he was leaving the house on his way into the office. The package had been delivered by FedEx special courier service, and the driver had informed her that explicit instructions were contained inside. She had opened the package right away and read the single-page letter addressed to her, which stated that only Mr. Irving Holmes was allowed to open the second envelope and he must be called without hesitation.

"The mysterious envelope! Oooh!" Irving chuckled. "But wait." He held up his index finger. "You did have the mailroom check it out to make sure there isn't a bomb in there!" he said in a playful tone. "I'm not trying to die today."

"I know, right?!" She shook her head. "But this envelope was delivered by FedEx. I think they check all their packages." She laughed. "But I patted the envelope just in case and didn't feel anything like wires."

She leaned across her desk and handed it to him. "It looks official."

Irving examined the envelope. "It does." He read his name typed across the front. "And there's no return address on the envelope or the FedEx package?" He glanced at the back flap.

"Nothing." She was anxiously waiting for him to open it. "Here's a letter opener." She slid a silver opener towards him.

"Thanks," he said before carefully sliding the opener under the top sealed flap.

"Here goes." He pulled free two single typed sheets of white linen paper and began reading.

Dear Mr. Irving Holmes and Mr. Brenner Gary,

After having a long, hard talk with myself and my best friend, Mae, I want to apologize again to you for my inappropriate behavior. I have never seen two people more in love than the two of you. I wish to honor your love and wedding with a gift in the amount of three million dollars, which is to be used to establish the Irving Holmes and Brenner Gary College Scholarship. Please see the enclosed check.

I ask that you set the eligibility criteria and the amount each student may receive and determine how the money should be managed. Most importantly, my name must remain anonymous.

My accountant has outlined instructions on the second page of this letter that you should share with Dr. Dalcoe and the board.

It is my hope you find my wedding gift an acceptable apology; also, I believe you will agree, that with this scholarship, many young boys will have the opportunity to go to college and excel in life. Hopefully, they, too, will find a true love just like the two of you!

Best regards, and may you be blessed with life, health, and happiness,
Mrs. Dorisse Glenn
Enclosed: A certified check

Chapter 47

"HEY, DAD!" RALPH SAID WITH YOUTH-
ful exuberance.

"Hey back to you! How's my boy doing?" Walt glanced at his calendar. He had his weekly Wednesday meeting in fifteen minutes, but
he knew he'd be late. Once a week, he joined the other executives for a
four-hour cabinet meeting.

"I'm cool, and all is good here in the A-town!"

Ralph was Walt and Helen's only child, and after graduating from
college, he had remained in Atlanta to work for a financial services
company.

"Good to hear. How's the job coming?"

"No complaints, and I really appreciate you helping me make those
connections. That made the difference."

"I just made a few phone calls. You're the one that nailed the
interview."

"I know, but without your calls, my resume would have just been
collecting dust like all the others."

"Well, I'm glad I was able to help. What do I owe the pleasure of your phone call to?" Walt chuckled.

Ralph laughed. "Why can't I just call my favorite dad to talk and see how you're doing?"

"You could, but my father antenna is up."

"Okay! You got me. Ahh..." Ralph paused and cleared his throat.

"Oh! Now you're pausing!" Walt teased. "Spit it out."

"Well, ahh, the reason for my call is to ask if I can get a loan of four thousand dollars so I can go with several of my friends to the Dominican Republic. There's this new resort down there right on the water, and we just want to hang out for five nights."

"Don't you have a job?"

"I do, Dad, but my savings is kinda light right now. But, I've already earned some vacation days, and counting the weekend, I'll have plenty of time."

"I see. Four grand sounds like a lot for five nights. Where are you staying? The Ritz?"

"It's not the Ritz," Ralph said with a chuckle, "but it's killer and I know how you and Mom want me to stay in nice places." Ralph feigned a logical tone. "This is a five-star-rated property and will cover my food, airfare, ground transportation costs, and activities."

"So, let me get this straight. You want to go on a trip but don't have any of the money? Don't you think this means you need to stay at home until you save the money?!"

Ralph laughed. "I know you want me to enjoy life," he teased. "Come on, Dad. Please???"

Walt laughed. "You're pouring it on thick!" He sighed knowing that he and Helen wanted only the best for their son. "I'll transfer the funds to your account today."

"Thanks, Dad! I love you, and you're the best father!"

"I love you more, son. Stay safe and be smart."

With a smile on his face, Walt deactivated the call and swiveled his chair around so he was facing his computer.

* * *

"Walt, should I let them know you'll be late for the meeting?" asked Rhyan Leaksville, his executive assistant, as she stood in the doorway.

She had worked for him for over five years. Though he was known as one of the smartest and most successful executives at the bank, she'd been told he could be difficult and arrogant. But he'd never been that way to her. Quite the opposite, in fact, and as a result, she loved working for him. He was supportive and kind, and he had become her mentor and ally.

"Please do, thanks. This shouldn't take more than fifteen minutes. I just need to make two calls." He looked at her briefly before turning back to his computer and jotting down the number.

"No worries! I'll give you some privacy." Rhyan reached for the doorknob. "Oh! Before I forget, the plant people are coming soon. Just in case you're in the meeting, I'll stay in here while they water your trees!"

She nodded at the huge Dracaena dorado plants, which flourished due to all the sunlight that filled his office.

"Thanks. I'll be sure to put anything confidential inside my drawer," he said, putting the phone receiver down. "You got a second? I want to ask your opinion."

"Sure thing." She released the knob. "Do you want me to close the door?" She hesitated, waiting for his response.

"That's not necessary. I'm going to send Helen flowers, probably roses. Do you think I should get half a dozen or a dozen?"

"Duh!" She rolled her eyes. "A dozen, of course! That's not even a question, Walt. And make them long stems." She smiled.

He chuckled. "I knew you were going to say that. I don't know why I even asked!" He gave her a thumbs-up. "A dozen long stems," he said before glancing at the florist's website.

"What's the occasion, if I might ask?"

He took a deep breath, reached in his pocket, and rubbed the dime. *Making up for a lot of shit, especially slapping her*, he wanted to say, but he didn't. "Let's just say I want to show my wife how special she is."

"Well, then, you betta' make it two dozen!!" She laughed and turned to leave. "Oh! And call Damani's Florist over on South Tryon Street. Not too far from the Mint Museum. She's been featured in *Essence*, Oprah's magazine, *Southern Living*, you name it!" Rhyan smiled as she waved her hands with excitement. "After she did the flowers for Serena's and Ciara's weddings, everybody wants her!"

"Got it! I'm calling right now," Walt said as he keyed in the information in the search engine.

"Okay, I'll let them know you're going to be late."

"Thank you, Miss Rhyan! Two dozen long-stem red roses it is," he said, watching as she closed the door.

He placed the order with Damani's Florist, paying extra for a before-noon delivery, and with that done, he made his second phone call.

Chapter 48

"WALT, HI! WHAT A PLEASANT SURPRISE. I haven't talked to you in a while."

Walt pushed his chair back and got to his feet. "Hello, Miss Myia Jordin! How've you been!?"

Making his way over to the floor-to-ceiling windows in his corner office, he gazed out, and from his vantage point, he could see all of downtown. People were walking in an unhurried pace, which was the norm.

Even when it rained, people in St. Winter leisurely strolled down its cobblestone streets. He and Helen had lived there since they'd gotten married. This was home, and he couldn't imagine living anywhere else.

"I've been good. How about you?" Myia said.

"Can't complain." He stepped back from the window and paced around his office.

I need to take Lennie on a trip, just the two of us, he thought, rubbing his left temple. *Get away for a couple of weeks. Maybe I could take her back to Jamaica and stay at that five-star resort she liked.*

"Are you looking for Helen? She's in her office," Myia said.

"Actually, I'm not calling to talk to her, but I was hoping you'd do me a favor." He slid his hand in his pocket. *It's been years since we've gone on a vacation that wasn't connected to my job or didn't include a group of friends.*

He sighed, wanting to kick himself. He thought about the many times Helen had wanted the two of them to stay longer or go somewhere by themselves. Each time, he'd said no.

At dinner the other evening, Noel hadn't answered any of his questions about his wife, not that he had expected her to, but she had confirmed one thing, that Helen wasn't the same person anymore. He had figured that much out, but he still had no proof of an affair. The only evidence of her change was a new wardrobe and attitude.

"You bet! Whatcha need?"

"I've ordered her some roses that should be delivered by lunchtime. As soon as they come, will you call me? I want to give her a call then." He was already thinking about what he would say to her.

He made his way back over to the window. *Later this week, I'm going to call a travel agent, get their help putting together a package for around Labor Day. I've got to make things right again.* He felt good about the progress they had made recently.

"Ahh!! More flowers!" Myia Jordin said in a girly tone. "Aren't you the romantic one. Two dozen black calla lilies a couple of weeks ago, and now roses. I'm impressed!"

Walt's eyes bulged, and he drew in a surprised breath. *What the fuck is she talking about?*

"Ah…ahh, the black calla lilies." His casual tone masked his confusion.

"She was on cloud nine when she got those flowers! They were gorgeous!"

"So…um, she liked them?" His mouth went bone dry. Not a drop of moisture remained.

"Liked them?! That's an understatement. She was so giddy that she floated the entire day!"

"Really?" His mind started racing. *What the fuck is a black calla lily?*

"Oh my gosh, yes! She loved them!"

Walt left the window and made his way over to his computer. Wedging the phone between his shoulder and ear, he pulled up Google. His fingers trembled as he typed in the words "black calla lily."

WHAT. THE. FUCK?! An icy chill rolled down his spine as the image of the flower popped up on the screen.

I knew it! She's having an affair! His pulse raced. *This isn't the type of flower a client would send. Too exotic, and they damn sure wouldn't send two dozen.*

Walt clinched his back molars as his temper ignited. *Damnit!*

He was having such a visceral reaction to what Myia Jordin had said that he was convinced his head would explode. As the hairs on the back of his neck stood, he stared at his computer.

The way she's been acting lately, I knew something was off. I knew it!

"And when I say she was floating, Helen was floating like her feet just wouldn't touch the ground! I know she's going to love the roses just as much!"

"Umm…ah," he stuttered, trying to get his words together. *Damn,* he thought as a sheen of perspiration dotted his forehead. He wiped his hand down his face and took a deep breath.

"Walt? You still here?" Myia asked after a long pause on his end.

She's having a fucking affair! I just knew it! Clients don't send black calla lilies. He breathed forcefully. *She's changed, alright,* he thought, remembering what Noel had said. *Fuck her, too,* he said to himself bitterly. *She knows that Helen's having an affair. She was probably laughing at me the entire night. Mocking me. Poor, stupid Walt, ha-ha. If he only knew.*

Looking around his office, he knew he couldn't afford to lose it while at work. He tried to rein in his temper but staring at the image of the calla lily wasn't helping.

"Walt?"

Shit. He breathed slowly as anger clouded his vision. "Yes…yes, I'm still here," he finally answered. Tension had taken up root in his head, and a severe headache was close by.

"Well, I hope she does like the roses as much as the black calla lilies," he said, feigning a pleasant tone, though he felt like he was about to throw up.

He put his hand in his pocket, buried it deep until he felt the dime. He started rubbing it, trying to calm down. *If a client did give them to her, which I know they didn't, she damn sure wouldn't be floating.*

"I'm sure she will!" Myia said with confidence. "What woman doesn't love getting flowers from her man!"

"You're right," he said. *But who is her man?* The question felt like a knife in his gut.

"So, I'll call you as soon as the flowers arrive. Okay?!"

"Thanks, Miss Jordin. You take care."

"You, too. Goodbye."

When the call ended, he pulled out his chair and plopped down.

"Damnit! Fuck! Helen, baby, no. Please, don't let it be true," he whispered as a toxic mix of misery, anger, and grief seeped through his pores, so thick that it nearly stopped his heart from beating.

He breathed deeply and sighed. "Helen, let me be wrong," he begged the heavens. "Please, baby, no," Walt whispered, but he already knew.

There was a soft knock at his door, but he didn't hear it.

Chapter 49

WALT HADN'T MOVED FROM HIS DESK, and his eyes had been glued to the ceiling. He'd been absorbed by his thoughts and immobilized for close to half an hour.

"Sorry to bother you," Rhyan said, sticking her head in the doorway. "Are you alright? You still going to the meeting?" She took a tentative step in and closed the door.

"Walt? Are you sick?" Concern crept in her tone when he did not respond or look at her.

After a long pause, he took a deep breath. "No, um...I..." He rubbed his hands down his face. "I'm fine. Really, I'm good."

He leaned forward and powered down his computer. "Listen, um..." Reaching inside his desk drawer, he pulled out his keys, locked his desk, and then locked his file cabinets.

"Walt, you're scaring me. Is everything alright?"

When she had left his office earlier, he had been upbeat, and this sudden change in his mood was jarring.

"Listen, um...I'm...um..." Without meeting her eyes, he quickly threw some papers on his desk into his briefcase.

Though his head was slightly bowed, she saw the pinched expression on his face.

"Walt, I'm getting worried. Do you want me to call the onsite nurse? It will just take a second for me to call her," she said, standing at the edge of his desk.

"No, I don't need the nurse," he said, controlling the look on his face. "But listen…something has come up, and I need to leave. I'll call Roderick and let him know I had an emergency."

While Walt didn't report to Roderick Brothers, he was one of the other senior executives at the bank who convened cabinet-level meetings. And since Walt was going to miss this meeting, he wanted to let him know.

"Oh my God, has anything happened to Helen or Ralph? Are they okay?" There was genuine panic in Rhyan's voice.

The sound of his wife's name elicited a glacial chill that ran down his spine like water, and he reached for the dime in his pocket and rubbed it. He took a deep breath. "Yes…um…they're fine. I just need to take care of an urgent matter. That's all."

"You sure?" She studied his face, still looking for clues.

"Yes, Rhyan, I'm sure. Something has come up. That's all." He came around his desk and stood next to her.

Seeing skepticism in her eyes, Walt intentionally changed his tone and demeanor to put her at ease. "I promise, Miss Rhyan. Now, stop worrying." He smiled.

Rhyan clasped her hands together. "Are you sure?"

"I'm sure. There are two things you can do for me, though."

"What's that? Just name it." She could see he was troubled, but she did not want to keep prying.

"Reschedule the plant people, and I want you to leave early as well."

She drew in a surprised breath. "Really! Are you sure?"

"Sure about the plant people or about you leaving early?" he teased, hoping to alleviate her concern.

Even though they kept things strictly professional, he had always been supportive of her, and she of him.

Rhyan chuckled. "You know what I mean!" She punched him in the arm.

"Oww!" he said playfully. "Yes, get out of here! I'm giving you permission to take the rest of the day off with pay! But be sure to lock my office." He headed towards the door.

She turned to watch him leave.

He knew she was watching him, and without turning around, he gave her one last reassurance. "Rhyan, I'm okay. Really. Just need to take care of something at home."

"Is there anything else you need me to do?"

Standing at the door, Walt said, "Yes. There are two more things you can do for me." He smiled. "First, stop worrying about me. I'm fine."

"And the second thing?" She plastered a smile on her lips that she didn't feel. In all the years she had known him, not once had he stuttered or seemed befuddled like he was today. Something was terribly wrong, and she knew it.

"Take the rest of the day off and have fun," he said before leaving.

Chapter 50

WALT'S MIND WAS SPLINTERED INTO fragments as images of his wife with another man taunted him.

Maybe she just has a secret admirer. He desperately wanted to believe that.

When he reached his car, he got in and locked the doors. He fastened his seatbelt and started the Lexus. Putting the car in reverse, he eased out of his reserved space.

Normally, he'd turn on the radio or listen to some music, but he did neither. There was too much going on in his head; he wouldn't hear it anyway.

He pulled up to the bank's parking gate and waved his hand at the security guard in the booth. When the heavy steel arm swung up, he drove through.

He adjusted his sunglasses before turning on his signal. Merging into the morning traffic flow, he headed down Main Street.

He had no destination in mind and was in no rush or hurry. He just knew he needed to clear his head before going home.

"Maybe I'm jumping to conclusions," he said, desperately trying to convince himself as he drove.

He needed to figure some things out. "There's got to be a logical explanation for the flowers." He sighed, pressing on the brakes as he approached the crosswalk.

A group of elementary children and three adults waited patiently for him and another car to stop.

Once it was safe to cross, the band of kids and women crossed the street. Laughing, giggles, and big smiles were all he saw as he watched the little ones hop, skip, and jump their way across as if walking were just too boring.

He realized they were headed to Betty's Bookstore when he saw the dozens of balloons taped to the door and the huge display window. The spectacle of balloons was a riot of color flapping in the wind.

When the light turned green, he eased down on the gas pedal.

His pulse started racing again. "Too many things are adding up, and my instincts are never wrong," he said with a strained voice.

That's the moment he let go, and sighed a sorrowful exhale as tears began to fall freely from his eyes.

"My wife is having an affair," he said in a broken whisper.

Chapter 51

HELEN WAS IN HER OFFICE, SITTING BE-
hind her desk, reviewing proposals from the top two finalists for the
social media services account, when her phone rang.

She couldn't help the smile that spread across her face upon seeing
the caller ID.

"Hi, Brenner." A sweetness was in her tone as she laid the proposal
down.

"Hello, my love. I hope I didn't call you at a bad time." His voice
was as smooth as aged brandy.

"It's never a bad time when you call. Besides, my next meeting isn't
for another half-hour. How are you?"

She got up from behind her desk and walked over to the window.
The muffled hum of an airplane that had taken off from the Charlotte
Douglas International Airport could be heard through the thick, insu-
lated office windows.

"I'm doing much better now that I am talking to you."

Through the glare of the sunlight, she gazed around the town's city-
scape, her eyes jumping from building to building until landing on the

bank. Walt's office window was on the top floor, in the corner facing her window. They used to joke, saying that with a pair of super-duper binoculars, they'd be able to spy on one another.

Is he looking at me now? she wondered as the vestiges of the kiss he'd given her before she'd left for work that morning tingled on her lips.

It was Walt's kisses, affection, and touch that she craved. To Helen, his touch was pure, uncut heroin. She was addicted to it, and he was her dealer.

"How are things coming with the wedding?" She stepped back from the window and slowly paced around her office.

"It's all coming together. We've got our tuxedos and the cake. The caterer is secured. The minister is confirmed. Flowers are ordered." He took a breath. "We're finalizing the photographer this week, and hopefully, the invitations are coming back from the printer this week."

"I'm impressed! You guys have practically done everything."

"That's what I keep telling my husband-to-be." Brenner laughed. "Irv's a nervous nelly, wanting things to be perfect."

As Helen listened to Brenner talk about his wedding, she was fully aware that what she'd done with them was wrong on every level. But all of the wrongness couldn't take away all of the rightness she felt at having these men be an indelible part of her. And if only through her memories, they would remain in her life forever.

She had decided not to go to Maui, as things between her and Walt were getting better, but she hadn't figure out how to tell Brenner. She was hoping he wouldn't mention the trip.

"I understand that," she said, running her fingers through her pixie-cut hair. "Only a perfect wedding is befitting a perfect couple."

"I'll tell Irving you said that. Did I mention that we're getting married in our backyard?"

"No, you didn't. That will make things easy."

"Exactly."

"How many people are you inviting?"

"The number keeps changing." He sighed. "First, it was forty. Now we might be up to sixty. I only wanted family, but Irv insisted on inviting friends and a few neighbors."

She laughed. "You know he's got you twisted around his little finger! His every wish is your command!"

"You're right. No denying that!"

"I've been thinking about what I'm going to get you guys for a wedding present."

She knew what she planned to give them; she only hoped she had enough time for it to be delivered before their big day.

"Baby, you've already given us our gift. Remember?" His sultry caress came straight through the phone lines.

"Aren't you the sweet-talker. Did you like your gift?" she whispered.

"*Mmm*, I loved it."

She smiled and made her way back to her desk, where she picked up her still-hot oolong tea, took a sip, and set her cup on the wooden coaster.

"Tell me, what's my love wearing today?" His voice dropped an octave. "I already know you look sexy as hell."

She threw her head back in a fit of laughter. "I know I've asked you this before, but are you sure you're still gay? Because you sound like a typical brother flirting."

"I am a typical brother flirting. Who is also gay."

"Okay, but gay brothers don't flirt with women."

"Gay brothers aren't blind, my love. We know a fine, sexy woman when we see one. And you are definitely one fine, sexy, and drop-dead-gorgeous woman," he said with a bit of machismo.

"Ooh! You're turning on the charm. I love it!" She leaned against the edge of her desk and crossed her arm over her stomach.

He chuckled low in his throat. "Yes, I am! Now, tell me. What are you wearing?"

She smiled and glanced down at her outfit. "I have on a pair of white linen capri slacks with a sleeveless white knit shell. I've got a wide chocolate belt on that has beige and white zebra stripes…"

Her voice trailed off when he said over her, "Sounds nice. Even though I'm imagining you with it off!"

"You just tryin' to get me in trouble by having me naked in the office. Not gonna happen." She chuckled.

"You're right! That might be a problem!"

"As I was saying before I was rudely interrupted, I also have on taupe suede wedge sandals." She glanced at her wrist. "And lots of slender gold bangles and a pair of long, eighteen-karat gold leaf earrings."

"Very, very nice. I wish I was there to see you in person."

She started pacing again. "So, what would you do if you were here?" she said softly.

"*Mmm*," he moaned, "what wouldn't I do?"

There was a knock at her door.

She glanced at the clock on the wall. It was eleven thirty.

"Brenner, hold on. Someone's at my door."

"No worries. I just wanted to hear your voice. I need to get ready for a meeting with a client, anyway."

"I'm so happy you called, because I wanted to hear your voice, too."

"Alright, my love. Have a great day."

"I will. You do the same, Brenner. Tell Irving I said hello."

They said their goodbyes and hung up.

"Come in," she said in a slightly raised voice.

Myia awkwardly opened the door.

Helen drew in a surprised breath, and her eyes widened. "Wow!!" she said, covering her mouth with her hands.

"These just came for you!" Myia exclaimed, walking in with the biggest bouquet of long-stem red roses that she had ever seen.

"Oh my goodness!! These are gorgeous!!" Helen said, quickly making a place for them on her desk.

Myia gently set the heavy vase down. "You're right! They are simply beautiful." She smiled and handed Helen the tiny envelope. "Here, this is for you."

"Thank you, Ms. Jordin."

The two women shared a smile as Helen anxiously tore open the envelope.

"They smell…" She paused and buried her nose deep within the folds of the luxurious silky blooms. She breathed in, filling her lungs with a fragrance that was as delicate as it was romantic. "Oh, my! These flowers are breathtaking! It looks like two dozen!" She pulled the small card free.

Myia chuckled. "I'm going to go now!" She wanted to call Walt, as he had requested.

"Okay! And thank you for bringing them in." She leaned against the edge of her desk. "Will you close my door, please?"

"Sure thing!" Myia said with a big grin on her face as she exited.

Helen looked down at the card and read the inscription.

You are my very best blessing. Please give me another chance.
Love, your husband

Chapter 52

RED ROSES WERE THE QUINTESSENTIAL flower of love and romance.

With this bouquet, Walt had made a statement, and his intentions were clear. He was affirming her importance in his life, professing his love, asking for another chance. He was boldly owning his failures and loudly asking her for forgiveness.

And in the past few days, he'd begun reigniting the embers of their passion with his toe-curling, soul-stirring, electrifying kisses and sweet, thoughtful gestures.

"Oh my God," she whispered as she gazed at the beautiful arrangement.

The white card was still in her hand, and she brought it closer and read the inscription again, though his words were already imprinted on her heart.

You are my very best blessing. Please give me another chance.
Love, your husband

Helen clutched the card to her chest as she walked around her desk and took a seat.

"I've got to call him!" Her voice rang with excitement.

She reached for her cell phone but dropped it when a cold chill ran down her spine.

"Damn," she said with a doleful sigh. "I just got off this phone with Brenner, damnit." There was a big knot of guilt in her throat that she had to either swallow or talk around because she absolutely wanted to call Walt now.

She took a deep breath, picked up her cell, and dialed his number. It went straight to voicemail. She dialed his office number. No answer.

"He must be in a meeting," she said, deciding to dial Rhyan's number. "I'm sure she can tell me when he'll be free."

Rhyan's voicemail message said she was taking the rest of the day off.

Helen sighed in frustration, "Let me text him," she said, disengaging from the call without leaving a message.

After she took a sip of tea, she slid back in her chair, set the cup on the coaster, and typed her text message.

WOW!!!!!!!!!!!! The roses r BEAUTIFUL!!!!!!!!!!!! And your card is Sooooo Wonderful! Can't wait to thank you in person. XOXOXO

She set her phone down and picked up the card. "You are my very best blessing. Please give me another chance. Love, your husband," she said in a hushed whisper.

Standing up, she leaned across her desk and pulled one of the long-stemmed flowers from the vase.

As she rubbed her fingers over the soft, velvety petals and breathed in the delicate yet provocative fragrance, a torrent of emotions filled her.

"Walt..." She breathed slowly. "God, please don't let him ever find out." Her eyes filled with unshed tears.

Taking a deep breath, she wiped away the tears that had begun to roll down her face like clear streams of pain and sorrow.

Holding the rose, she stood and walked to the window.

Noel said he has suspicions about me having an affair. She glanced down at the people walking along Main Street. *But he has no proof. Just suspicions. Walt can't find out now! He just can't. Not when things are beginning to get back on track for us. I will always love Brenner and Irving. But it's time for things to come to an end. No trip to Maui, and somehow I've got to figure out a way to tell them to stop calling me. Let them live their lives. Because I want to dedicate myself to my husband and my marriage.*

She took a deep breath, trying to settle the butterflies fluttering around her insides, and turned away from the window. *Walt will never find out,* she thought, trying to convince herself.

"I'll keep it that way," she said, making her way back to her desk, where she finished the last of her oolong tea.

That day with Brenner and Irving, she'd given herself permission to do what she absolutely wanted to do and freed herself from anything and everything.

"But that's all behind me now." And with a peculiar ease, Helen was ready to put the matter of her affair aside, to just sweep her betrayal under the rug like it was an insignificant matter.

Now, li'l missy, dis ain't no small thang. You don' fucked two men! The old-lady voice chuckled. *You can't sweep a heap of shit like dat under da rug and 'spect it not to stink up the whole house! A pile dat high gon' trip you up, sho nuf, one of dese days!*

Helen brought the rose to her nose and inhaled. Steeling her spine, she sat back down, determined to ignore the old lady's banter.

"Things are so good between us now," she said with a sigh before glancing at the clock on the wall.

Her meeting was in ten minutes.

She breathed in the perfume of the red bloom again, thinking how perfect and luxurious the flowers were.

Looking at her text messages, she noticed that Walt had not responded.

"He must be busy. Let me try him one more time."

She called his cell phone but got no answer. She then called his office number. It went straight to voicemail.

She dialed Rhyan's office number and got her voicemail.

"I'll text him again," she said, typing another message.

Hey, Im loving the roses!!!! Pls call me or text when u r free! Love, H

She took a deep breath, laid the phone down, and gathered the presentation materials from her desk.

With a look of nostalgia on her face, Helen opened the door, and as she made her way down the hall to her next meeting, her mind had convinced her the affair would remain a secret.

"Everything is going to be just fine," she whispered.

Chapter 53

WALT ENTERED THE HOUSE WITH AN IN-terior pain so foul that its stench permeated the air.

After leaving work, he'd needed to think. Going no place in particular, he'd driven around for hours as images of his wife with another man played a game of hitting the piñata with his mental psyche. Instead of candy dropping out, the images caused his pulse to beat faster and faster.

For the life of him, he just couldn't fathom how things had gotten so bad between them, but she'd changed too drastically for it to be the result of a secret admirer.

Only the attention of a new lover could bring about the changes he had seen: the sway of her hips, her different walk, the way she acted, her brand-new wardrobe, and the way she talked to him.

He punched in the four-digit code to deactivate the alarm and dropped his keys in the basket on the counter by the butler's pantry door.

Where is she? he wondered bitterly, though he knew that unless she was having dinner with Noel, she usually got in around five forty-five, and it was only five twenty-five.

He kicked off his black wingtips, pulled his light gray dress shirt out of his pants, and unbuttoned the top four buttons.

He didn't bother turning on any lights or music as he made a bee-line through the kitchen to the keeping room and then straight to the minibar.

With each of his footfalls, as if sensing his mood, the house grew still and quiet and held its breath.

He rolled up his sleeves, reached underneath the minibar's wooden cabinet, picked up one of the Baccarat Harmonie whiskey glasses, and set it on the small countertop.

A sub-zero refrigerator built into one of the cabinet drawers stored the ice cubes, and when he opened the drawer, a rush of cold air hit his face. Using long silver tongs, he scooped out two ice cubes and dropped them in the glass.

Clink. Clink.

He set the tongs aside, picked up a bottle of Jack Daniels, and un-screwed the top.

The world-famous Tennessee whiskey had come about when an en-slaved black man and master distiller by the name of Nathan "Nearest" Green had taught Jack Daniels how to distill, and if it hadn't been for Mr. Green, Walt would've been drinking another whiskey.

"Where is she?" He let out a slow, languid breath as he poured three ounces of the golden-brown liquid for a double. Its heady aroma tempted and teased his nose.

Re-screwing the top, he set the whiskey bottle on the counter, picked up a can of Coke, popped the top, and poured in about two tablespoons. He used a bar spoon to mix his drink, stirring it to his satisfaction.

With the drink in his hand and his moodiness coiled around him like a vice, he went into the sunroom and set the drink on the small wicker table. Feeling like the weight of the world was on his shoulders, he collapsed on the white wicker furniture, then picked up the glass and brought it to his lips and took a generous sip of his Jack and Coke.

"She's fucking somebody," he said, yearning to be wrong but knowing he wasn't.

His head throbbed and he laid it back against the cushions and closed his eyes, hoping to soothe his head, his heartache, and the rampant pain and misery that had found a home inside of him. And he desperately hoped to soothe his bruised and bloodied ego.

After a long, long moment, the low hum of a lawnmower starting up down the street broke through his silent agony.

He opened his eyes, leaned forward, and glanced at his watch. It was five forty-five.

"Where is she?" he said before taking a big sip. Settling back, he put his sock-covered feet on the rattan ottoman.

"Damn sure no client sent her black calla lilies," he said angrily. "I wonder what lie she'll tell me when I confront her?"

He swirled his drink around, and the chunky ice cubes clanked against the chilled sides.

He exhaled in anguish, lifted the whiskey glass to his lips, and took a generous sip of his drink. Its smooth, rich heat eased down his throat and tried its best to coax his nerves back from the edge of the cliff from which they were dangling.

Breathing deeply, Walt took another generous sip of his Jack and Coke, then another, and another.

Chapter 54

THE GARAGE DOOR TRUNDLED UP, AND the jarring clanking sound registered like a symphony to his ears. It meant she was home.

Walt opened his eyes and glanced at his watch. It was six thirty.

He brought the whiskey glass to his lips and drained it dry. It was his third drink.

His headache had worsened from all of the alcohol that he'd poured into his unfed stomach, and the veins in his head felt as taut as tightropes.

He had been rooted in the same spot since getting home, except for when he'd gotten up to make his Jack and Cokes and go to the bathroom to let out streams of whiskey-tinged pee.

He exhaled, leaned forward, and set the glass on the wicker table. Then, with a listless drunkard's plop, he sat back and waited for her.

The garage door closed.

When he heard the door to the house open, he breathed deeply, and using his index fingers, he massaged his temples up and down with long, fluid movements, hoping to loosen the tension.

Helen came in and placed her car keys in the basket on the counter. The house was quiet, and she assumed Walt was watching CNN.

With her hands full, she carefully set the small flower vase on the counter first. Her purse and briefcase were still in the car. She'd get them later.

Before she'd left work, she'd decided to bring half a dozen of the roses home and leave the rest in her office. This way, she could enjoy the beautiful flowers in both places.

Walt heard her moving around the kitchen, but he said nothing as he continued to massage his temples.

She slid out of her wedge sandals and left them by the door.

Making her way over to the breakfast table, she placed the yellow and white polka-dot gift bag on the table. Then she walked to the stove, where she set the brown take-out bag with two dinners from Fuzzy's.

Turning away from the stove, that's when she saw him sitting in the sunroom.

"Oh! You scared me!" she said, startled. "I thought you were upstairs. Why didn't you say something?"

Ever since getting his flowers and reading his card, she'd been simply euphoric. She walked into the sunroom with a huge smile on her face and her arms stretched out wide, ready to give him a big hug.

"Walt, thank you for my beauti—"

Her words died on her lips, and she drew up short at the scowl on his face and the coldness that seeped from him.

"Where have you been?"

"Is everything alright?" she asked cautiously as she came to stand in front of him.

He raked his eyes down her body in such a way that it felt crude, and it rattled her.

She took in a settling breath. Her first assumption was that his mood had to be work related.

"I ASKED you a question." The look in his eyes was venomous. "Where have you been?" His tone commanded an answer.

She wrung her hands, and her eyebrows scrunched up. "Walt, is everything okay?" she said, glancing at the empty whiskey glass on the table.

He let out a loud and weary gush of air.

And she got a good whiff of the alcohol on his breath.

He's drunk, she realized, noticing how glassy his eyes were. She wondered if he had even blinked since she'd been standing there.

Walt cocked his head to the side. "Why don't you answer my question?" he said with a vicious bite.

She felt nervous all of a sudden. "I...I went to Betty's Bookstore and got a gift for Myia's niece. Her birthday party is tomorrow." She swallowed, feeling a dryness in her mouth. "And I stopped by Fuzzy's and got us something to eat."

She glanced towards the kitchen. "I left it on the stove." Looking back at him, she asked, "Walt, is everything okay?"

He looked at her with a hard and unsettling gaze, as if he were trying to see past her skin, all the way to her skull.

Her knees wobbled, but she took a deep breath and tried to ignore her wariness. She smiled, pretending not to notice his mood. "Walt, I called your cell like ten times today to thank you for my beautiful flowers! They're absolutely gorgeous!"

Helen leaned down and gave him a kiss on his cheek. She smelled the alcohol on his breath even more now with her being this close, but she said nothing. "I kept getting your voicemail." She threw her hands up playfully in mock defeat. "I texted you several times, too. You never called or sent a text."

The upbeat tone of her voice was at odds with how she felt. "Did something happen at the bank today? Is that why I didn't hear from you?" She was still trying to figure out why he was in such a dark funk.

Walt had seen every one of her calls, watched her name displayed across his phone's screen. He'd had no intention of answering her calls or responding to her texts.

When he just stared at her, raking his eyes down her body, she talked to fill in the awkward moment. "And the card…" she said in a wistful tone and touched her heart. At the memory of the words he'd written, a smile lit up her face. "It was the best part of all. It was so special. Thank you so, so much! You made my day!"

He just looked up at her, and when his eyes turned from cold to frigid, she trembled on the inside.

She took a deep breath and flapped her hands like waving a white flag.

"Okay. Let me leave you alone. I can tell you're in a bad mood. I'm going to get out of your way. I will put your food in the oven to keep it warm and take mine upstairs and eat in the bedroom."

She tugged on the bottom edges of her sleeveless white top. There was no reason to do that; she just felt the need to do something with her hands other than wringing them again.

He remained silent as he looked at her.

Their gazes locked for a moment before he rubbed his hands down his face.

His temper was simmering, and he wanted another drink. Now that he'd learned about the calla lilies and her reaction to them, it all made sense and this bit of information was the proof he needed.

Without a shred of doubt, he knew she'd violated their sacred bond. She had disregarded all the good they'd built over nearly thirty years. And if he were jumping to conclusions, he knew he'd jumped to the right one.

He took a deep breath, picked up his glass, stood, and came around the wicker table until he was mere inches from her.

"So, you liked your flowers, huh?"

The smell of whiskey teased her nose as she looked up at him from her petite height. At six feet, he stood a whole foot taller than her.

"Yes! I told you they were gorgeous! Absolutely gorgeous! And the card was so special. I'm keeping it in my wallet." She smiled, but her pulse was racing. There was something about him that unnerved her.

"Let me ask you this, wife." He reached out and brushed aside a strand of her hair.

She feigned a bravado that she didn't feel. "What do you want to ask me, husband?" she said, putting her hand on her hip.

He slid his hand from her hair to under her chin. Looking into her eyes, he stroked her skin softly.

He wanted to see the nuanced changes in her expression, no matter how slight, how minute. He needed to see her eyes, needed to see if there was a shred of guilt or remorse.

He lifted her chin a bit higher, and with a menacing calm in his voice, he locked his eyes on hers and like a snake slithering in the grass, Walt was ready to strike.

"Did you like your roses better than the black calla lilies?"

Shit, she thought as a freezing chill ran through her body, and it took everything in her not to look away.

She opened her mouth, but nothing came out.

Chapter 55

"CAT GOT YOUR TONGUE?"

Her heart was beating like a drum, and she feared he would hear it thumping in her chest.

She swallowed and feigned a look of innocence. "Of course, the roses, but who told you that I got black calla lilies?"

"Don't worry about that. Who sent you the flowers? And please don't insult my intelligence by telling me they came from a client," Walt said, looking her dead in the eyes.

They were standing impossibly close, with not an inch between them. If he hadn't been holding her chin, she'd have looked away.

Helen knew he had suspicions about her having an affair, but how had he gotten information about the calla lilies?

Keeping her face composed, she tried to quickly come up with a logical explanation.

"As a matter of fact, they did come from a client, one who is trying to get our social media account," she said convincingly, but beneath her feigned calm composure, she was deeply worried.

He chuckled low in his throat. *Damn, she's lying with a straight face,* he thought, but he said nothing, just kept looking at her. *She's concocting a web of lies in her head right now, I'll bet.*

"Listen, I'm hungry…" She gently eased his fingers from underneath her chin.

He smirked as he slid his hand into his pocket.

Her heart pounded. "I can tell you're in a bad mood, so I'm going inside." Her tone was light, and she desperately wanted to look away from him, but she didn't. Thought it would make her look guilty.

"Can you STOP LYING and tell me the truth?"

The sarcasm in his tone caused an army of butterflies in her stomach.

"Walt, I told you the truth. They came from a client. Now, I'm leaving." She turned and eased away from his unsettling glare.

With lightning speed, he grabbed her arm.

Her eyes widened as she gasped. "Why are you grabbing me!?!"

"I TOLD YOU NOT TO INSULT my intelligence by telling me those flowers came from a client. No client would send you something like that unless you're fucking them!"

"LET GO!" she shouted, trying to free herself from his hold. "You're DRUNK!" she spat out.

His grip tightened.

"I said LET go of ME!" She squirmed and glared up at him.

He quickly loosened his grip.

She snatched her hand away. Her face flushed, and she rolled her eyes at him before stomping off to the kitchen.

He chuckled. "I hit a nerve, didn't I?" His eyes roamed down her backside, "That's why you runnin'?"

He watched her hips and butt sway.

Her heart was literally in her throat, beating a frantic rhythm, and she did not turn around or stop walking, just continued into the kitchen. But she felt the heat from his body because, like a stalker, he was right behind her.

"Walt, leave me alone," she said over her shoulder. "You're DRUNK, and I'm not interested in having a confrontation with you!" She gritted her teeth.

"We don't have to have a confrontation." He laughed, knowing that he'd cornered her. "Just tell me the truth about who sent you the flowers. Are you fucking them?"

"Like I said, you're drunk, and I'm not interested in smelling whiskey all night," she said in a mocking tone.

What Helen had hoped would never happen was happening right now, and the mask of innocence that she had worn was beginning to crack.

Chapter 56

MEANWHILE, ACROSS TOWN IN CHARLOTTE, a different energy flowed through Irving and Brenner's home. An instrumental jazz tune played softly, and the couple was getting ready for dinner.

"Can you believe the gift we got from Dorisse?!" Irving said, amazed at Dorisse's generosity. "I think I like her now." He chuckled and set a basket of hot dinner rolls on the dining room table.

"I can't get over it!" Brenner uncorked a bottle of red wine and filled his glass halfway. "Three million dollars to fund a scholarship in our names!"

"Imagine that," Irving said, pulling out his chair and sitting down. "The Irving Holmes and Brenner Gary Scholarship. It has a nice ring to it, don't you agree?"

"It absolutely does. Tell me when?" Brenner poured the deep-burgundy wine in Irving's glass.

"That's good."

Brenner handed Irving his glass, leaned down, and kissed him on the lips before taking a seat at the other end of the table. "Dinner smells good."

It was Irving's turn to cook, and he'd prepared a casserole with con-chiglioni shells, spinach, bacon, ricotta cheese and heirloom tomatoes, along with a garden salad.

"Thank you, baby." Irving smiled.

After saying grace, the couple leaned across the table and clinked glasses.

"I hope it's good." Irving scooped a heaping portion onto Brenner's plate and then his.

"I'm sure it is. Plus, I'm starving." Brenner accepted his plate and then reached inside the basket for a roll.

"Well, there's plenty." Irving took a bite. "*Umm*, this is yummy, if I do say so myself!" He danced in his seat, and after swallowing, he took a sip of wine. "So, how was your day?"

"This casserole is tasty. You nailed it!" Brenner said as he forked up another bite. "My day was good. I spent most of it in disposition, but during a break, I called Helen. She said hello."

"And did you tell my queen about Maui?"

Brenner sighed. "No. I couldn't bring myself to do it. The time didn't feel right."

Irving waved his hand in diva-esque mode, "Well, chile, don't wait until the day we're leaving to go on our honeymoon. You got this." He sliced a cucumber from his salad and popped it in his mouth.

"There's no need for you to worry. I'll figure it out." Brenner blew Irving a kiss. "How was your day?"

"My day was fine. Listen. Changing the subject, you know what I've been thinking?"

"What's that?"

"About the song I'll walk down the aisle to."

"What about it?" Brenner took a sip of wine.

"Well, the traditional 'Here Comes the Bride' just ain't it for me." Irving laughed and used air quotes. "I was thinking about doing something more modern, more us."

"We're definitely a modern couple." Brenner smiled.

"How about the song 'Just Because' by Anita Baker. You know, I love you just because, just because I do, my darlin' you," he sang.

"I love it!"

"I love it, too! It's perfect, right?" Irving bit into a roll. "If we can't find a singer, I'm okay having the DJ play the record as I walk down the aisle."

"I cannot wait!"

"Because you know I can walk, honey." Irving snapped his finger.

"You're so sexy right now."

"Yes, and I'm going to strut down the aisle and claim my man." Irving's smile lit up his face.

Chapter 57

HELEN KNEW WALT WAS ON HER HEELS, but when he suddenly turned her around and pressed her against the butler's pantry door, sandwiching her between his toned, muscular body and the wooden rigidness of the door, she yelped.

"WHAT ARE YOU DOING?" she shouted, looking him dead in the eye as her chest rose and fell with anxious breaths.

Seeing the drunken, heated look in his eyes caused her heart to skip a beat, and before she knew what he was doing, he grabbed her by the wrists and suspended them high above her head.

Her eyes widened in surprise as his big, masculine hand held both of her wrists together like it was child's play. But it wasn't, as she failed to break his hold.

"STOP! What are you doing?" she demanded, trying to wrestle free.

He clenched his teeth and looked into her eyes. "NOW, I'm going to ask you this one more time…"

"Walt, you're DRUNK!" she said bitterly, smelling the alcohol on his breath. "LET GO of me! I mean IT!" She squirmed and bucked, twisting right and left.

The white knit top she was wearing rose, showing a thin ribbon of her caramel-colored stomach.

She glared at him as her exertion did little to move him. She took a deep breath and swallowed. Trying to calm down.

"Walt, I told you the truth about the flowers." Her voice was cajoling. "They came from a client who wants to win our social media account. And no, I'm not sleeping with them."

Helen frequently swallowed whenever she was nervous or telling a lie. It was a telltale sign that he had noticed many years ago.

"You know, when you've been with someone as long as we have, you develop a keen sense about that person," he said with a quiet edge to his voice, "Kind of like a sixth sense. You can tell if they've had a bad day. A good day. You can even tell when they're lying. Like you are."

"I'm not lying."

He shook his head in disbelief and then looked down at her breasts and her stomach. He watched the adrenaline rush through her and then slowly lifted his gaze to meet her eyes.

Under his harsh glare, she felt jittery and unstable.

"Helen, I SWEAR to God…" He ground his back molars; his restraint on his temper was slipping by the second.

"Walt, I'm telling you the truth. I went out to dinner with the client, and they sent me flowers to say thank you. I guess they picked the calla lilies to make an impression." Her mouth felt as dry as a desert, and she swallowed, trying to moisten it.

He locked his eyes on hers like two magnets, and his breath became labored as his nostrils flared in anger. "If you keep lying to me…" He exhaled a loathing rush of air.

She saw the look in his eyes, could feel his body tense up like he was riding a lightning rod and was about to explode.

Suddenly he wedged his right leg between hers, forcing her to straddle his thigh.

"Now, tell me…" He paused, and the simmering tension seeping from his pores hung in the air. "Look at me, Lennie." He lifted her chin high with his index finger. "You tell me the truth."

Her pulse raced impossibly faster.

"Just answer the question, and you better not utter another lie."

He tightened his grip on her wrists. "Are you fucking somebody?"

Just saying these words made Walt want to throw up.

Helen took a deep breath and forged her spine with steel, knowing that of all the questions in the world, this one was the one she dreaded most.

Ain't no reason to lie now, missy, 'cause he can smell yo' shit a mile away. Fess up. You grown, ain't cha? said the old-lady voice.

"ANSWER ME, DAMNIT!!!"

His loud voice startled her, and a bit of whiskey-tinged spit splattered her nose.

He'd become unhinged. "OPEN YOUR MOUTH AND ANSWER ME," he yelled. "ARE YOU FUCKING SOMEBODY?"

She gazed into his chocolate-brown eyes. They were clouded with pain and barely controlled rage. Then she took in his handsome face. She'd forever adore it, but it was now shadowed by a sadness she had put there.

"ANSWER ME, HELEN!"

The veins on the sides of his neck bulged, and she felt his stomach rise and fall with his anger.

Answer tha man, missy. And don't lie. You did what you did, said the voice of her inner counselor.

"OPEN YOUR MOUTH AND ANSWER ME!!" The smell of whiskey on his breath was strong.

Helen trembled, and she felt breathless as her eyes pooled with tears.

Open yo' mouth and answer the man, missy. Tell him da truth. You's be free.

Walt's pulse quickened as he watched Helen's eyes.

Even with her teary eyesight, she could see his anger, pain, and frustration. His grief and sadness were so vivid that it was her undoing, and it took everything in her not to look away.

She met his eyes and then watched his face crumble as the raw agony of what he knew she was about to say tore through him.

Walt watched the tears roll down her beautiful face, and he sighed wearily as he loosened his hold on her wrists. "Are you having an affair?" he said softly.

In a broken whisper, she confessed, "Y…ye…yes."

Chapter 58

HER "YES" WAS A BLADE THAT SLICED through his heart, stopping it from beating. Not figuratively, but literally.

Walt was stunned. Everything inside of him shut down as if lightning had struck his internal power grid. All he could do was stare at the woman in front of him. He no longer recognized her; she was a stranger, or maybe someone he vaguely knew.

Instinctively knowing the truth and hearing it said out loud were two entirely different things. Hearing it meant you could no longer pretend you were overreacting or jumping to conclusions.

The truth was out, and there was no going back. She could not unspeak the word, nor could he un-hear the word that he had just heard.

"Walt," Helen whimpered, "I'm so...sor...sorry." Guilt clung to her like a dry, itchy layer of skin.

Without warning, he stepped back, letting go of her like he had no right to even touch her.

"Walt, plea...please," she whispered, reaching her hands out to him.

The look of devastation and despair on his face ripped through her. "I'm sorry. I'm sor...sorry." She cried as fresh tears rolled from her eyes.

He'd never been able to stomach her crying. This was killing him, but he ignored her tears as he stepped further and further away.

She rubbed her wrists and took tentative baby steps towards him.

"DON'T," he said forcefully, moving out of her reach. *I knew it*, he thought. *I just knew it.*

"Plea...please," she said in a shaky timid voice.

He walked away from her, over to the doorway leading upstairs. He was struggling with an anger and confusion so deep that he felt like he'd been plunged into an abyss.

Standing at the doorway, he took a deep breath, bowed his head, and rubbed his temples.

Knowing that his wife had betrayed him, cuckolded him, created cracks and crevices for seeds of hate to inch their way into his heart.

"It would be easy for me to hate you right now. Hate you for breaking our vows and letting another man fuck you," he said harshly.

"I'm so...sorry. I'm sorry, Walt," she said, sniffing in the snot running from her nose.

She took a tentative step towards him.

"I told you, DON'T COME NEAR ME." He seethed as his eyes ran down her body with a look of disgust.

Why, Helen? he asked himself.

"I won't. I'll stop right he...here," she said softly. Leaning against the stove, she wiped away her tears as more flowed.

He sighed in misery. "Can I ask you something?" he said, feeling an emotional storm brewing inside his stomach. One minute, he tasted pure hate for her, and the next, he felt only unconditional love.

She wiped her eyes, and when she looked at him, she saw the tears in his. "Yes." Her voice was soft, hesitant.

"Did you like how he fucked you? Did he fuck you like a slut? Like his whore?"

As if he held a pair of scissors in his hand and were cutting away pieces of his own soul, Walt paid a heavy toll just saying these words to his wife.

She said nothing.

After a moment, he shook his head. Every nerve in his body felt charred.

As he turned to leave, he gave her one last look. She read it as a look of hate, and as the ugly devastation of what she'd done sank in, it destroyed her.

Tears ran from her puffy, swollen eyes like rivers filled with sorrow, and she crumbled to the floor like a ragdoll with cotton-filled legs.

Chapter 59

IT WAS MIDNIGHT, AND THE AIR IN THE house was stagnant as remnants from their heated argument drifted from room to room like specters.

Walt had breathed in the stagnant air as he tossed and turned in bed all night. Finally, he gave up. He'd been haunted by Helen's face, the tears in her eyes, and her sad, weepy voice.

He took a deep breath, sat up, and glanced at the clock on his nightstand.

He then looked over at her side of the bed. Aided by the glow from the nightlight by the door, he could tell she wasn't there. The bedcover was as smooth and undisturbed as it had been that morning.

"She's probably in the guest bedroom," he said, but moments later, he berated himself for caring. *Why should I give a damn where she's at*, he thought bitterly. "Hell, she might have left to be with him."

He stared at the ceiling, feeling agitated as his mind replayed that evening. "Damnit." He sighed, remembering the moment she had confessed.

I knew something wasn't right, that something had changed about her. I could feel it. Telling me the flowers came from a client. Bullshit! He sighed loudly. *A client your ass slept with.*

Lying there, he carried on such a vigorous conversation in his mind that he felt his head would explode.

He glanced at the clock. It was four minutes past the last time he'd looked.

He pushed the covers back and swung his legs over the side, bringing his weary self to a sitting position. He sat there, wondering how things had gotten so bad.

"Damn," he huffed. *What do I do now? She might still be with the dude.* He got goosebumps at the thought. *For all I know, she could've fucked him today.*

He stood up and made his way to the bathroom, wondering what had happened to his neat, orderly world. It was as if a category four hurricane had blown through his life, leaving behind total destruction, disarray, and upheaval.

Moments later, he flushed the toilet and washed and dried his hands.

He returned to the bed, and as if a beacon were drawing his eyes to her side, he glared at the spot where, for nearly thirty years, night after night, she'd lain beside him, sleeping and dreaming.

But she was not there. Not now.

He stood at the foot of the bed, staring at her side, "Why, Lennie? Why didn't you come to me first and give us a chance to work things out?"

As soon as the words left his mouth, he felt a hard punch to his gut, remembering an evening not that long ago when she had tried to seduce him and the hurt and embarrassment in her eyes when he had turned her away.

He sighed, rubbed his hands down his face and decided a drink of water might help him settle down and make sleep come a little easier.

Walt descended the stairs, and when he came into the kitchen, he did not expect to see what he saw.

Chapter 60

THE ONLY LIGHT ON WAS THE ONE ABOVE the stove, but it provided enough illumination for him to see.

Surprised that she was on the floor, "I…ah…" He cleared his throat.

A heap of mess she was, huddled against the stove, with her legs drawn tightly against her chest and her arms wrapped around her knees.

She had been in that spot for hours, and it was obvious to him that she had not slept a wink, as if she'd been robbed of any respite.

Silently Helen watched him, but she said nothing, just followed him with her sad eyes.

Her makeup was completely ruined, and he had never seen her look so pitiful, uncertain, and broken; quite frankly, he did not know what to think.

He grabbed a clean glass from the cabinet, walked to the refrigerator, pressed the water dispenser on the outside panel, and filled his glass.

He felt her eyes follow him.

And out the corner of his eye, he glanced down at her and realized he did not want to leave. There were burning questions he needed answers to.

With the glass of water in his hand, he walked over to the counter opposite her and leaned against it.

His black pajama pants rode low on his waist, and since he wasn't wearing the matching top, she got a good look at his tone abs and obliques.

"Walt…" Her voice was a thin whisper as she unfolded her legs. She breathed in. "I am so sorry."

He just looked at her.

The sadness in her tone was tearing his heart apart, but he held his tongue, watching as she stiffly got up off the floor.

In all things, in all ways, and always, make love, he heard Mrs. Bennett's voice.

But how can I do this now? He gazed at his wife over the rim of his glass. *Certainly, this rule doesn't apply when your wife is fucking another man.* He thought before taking a big sip of water.

She wanted to touch him, but she feared he'd tell her to get back, so she stood against the stove.

He took another sip of water and then set the glass on the granite countertop. When he turned around, he rubbed his hands down his face and took a deep breath.

After a long pause, he said, "Can I ask you something?"

"Ye…yes. Certainly." Her voice wobbled as she wiped away a tear.

"Was I that bad of a husband?"

Her eyes widened. "No, no, Walt." There was a vulnerability in his voice that she had not heard before, and it surprised her.

"You're not a bad husband. Not at all. I beg you, please don't think that," she said softly.

"Then why?"

She sighed. "You know, there's no excuse for what I did. I think I just got so upset with where my life was that I wanted to do something for me," she said softly as tears filled her eyes. "But I should have tried harder to get things back on track with us, and for that, I will never forgive myself."

He closed his eyes, breathed in, made an "o" with his lips, and exhaled. He did it again, releasing tiny amounts of anger, frustration, and pain.

When he spoke, his voice cracked. "It's my fault, Lennie. I pushed you a...way. I've been such a fool for so many years."

He felt sick on the inside. *I stopped taking care of you, and you went looking for attention from another man.* "I know I messed up," he said around a sob.

Surprised by his tears and what he was saying, her own heart filled with sadness.

"Walt..." Without thinking, she rushed over, put her arms around his waist, and said a silent prayer when he did not move away and allowed her to touch him. "No. It's not all your fault. I pushed you away, too."

Her voice held not only the heavy burden of her guilt, but also a lightness from a glimmer of hope.

Chapter 61

WALT CLEARED HIS THROAT, WIPED HIS eyes, and took a deep breath. "Are you still seeing him?" He slid his hands into the pockets of his pajama pants.

"No, I'm not." She met his eyes. *Although I've been talking to them and had plans to fly out to Maui.*

It was not a lie. It was true that she had not seen Brenner or Irving since their date.

"I mean, I don't want to make a fool out of myself, thinking that… um…" He took a breath.

"Walt, I'm not." To think that someday she'd have to tell him that it was not one man, but two. Would that fact make a difference? Would that be too much for him to accept?

He looked into her eyes. "Do you want to…see him? I mean, would you rather be with him?"

There was an uncertainty in his voice that tugged on her heartstrings.

"I…ah better not make any assumptions."

Helen tightened her arms around his waist and laid her head against his bare chest. "I want you. Only you, Walt," she whispered, feeling his heartbeat against her face.

"Are you sure? Or do you really want him? Tell me," he pleaded in a quiet voice.

Brenner's and Irving's handsome faces whispered across her mind. The memory of that day would live inside of her for the rest of her life. And while she truly loved them, without a doubt, she knew who she wanted.

"I am absolutely sure," she said with clear certainty.

Walt remembered Dr. Bennett's advice and breathed in a resolve that he didn't know he had. Could he swallow his pride and coax his battered ego into doing the impossible by forgiving her?

"Then end it, Lennie. Call that motherfucker tomorrow and end it!" His tone was stern.

She lifted her chin and met his eyes. "Yes, yes, I will," she said quickly.

"I mean IT! First thing."

"Yes." There was a softness in her tone. "First thing in the morning. It's done. It's over."

Her breath caught in her throat as a wave of fresh tears bubbled up. "Walt, will yo…you for…give me?" She laid her head on his chest and started crying.

"Shh, stop. You know it kills me when you cry."

She wiped away her tears, put her head back against his solid body, and felt grateful that he had not pushed her away. She took this as solace.

"You've broken my heart into a thousand pieces and left a gigantic hole inside of me that I don't think will ever close…" He paused. "And I don't think I'll ever forget how badly you hurt me, but regardless of what you say, I will always feel that this is my fault, that I pushed you away."

After a brief pause, he added, "But somehow we'll get past this. It's not going to be easy. There will be a lot of days and weeks when I'm not going to want to see you, and I might just stay at a hotel or sleep in the guest bedroom."

He sighed with a heaviness that weighed him down. "This is a lot, Lennie, and while I might have pushed you away, I'm not going to lie. It will take everything in me to recover from you being with another man, and truthfully, I don't know if I ever will. Not fully, anyway."

He felt her wet, silent tears roll down his stomach.

"You're crying again, aren't you?" he said softly.

She nodded as she wiped her eyes.

"We're going to get through this. But we'll need the very best marriage counselor that money can buy." He took a deep breath. "It's been a long, brutal day. Let's go to sleep and climb this mountain tomorrow."

"Will you forgive me?" she whispered.

When he did not respond, she said, "Walt? Did you hear me?"

"I heard you."

"Do you think you can forgive me?"

He breathed in and blew out a long breath of air. "Right now, I'm feeling too raw to answer that question, but ask me again in the morning."

"I understand," she whimpered and wiped her eyes. "I love you, Walt."

"I love you, too, Helen Charlena Gothrock."

He took her hand, and they silently walked up the stairs. By the time Helen had showered and gotten into bed, Walt was sound asleep.

Chapter 62

IT WAS THURSDAY MORNING AT EIGHT.

Helen felt as though a heavy wind and rain had pounded the earth all night for hours, and left behind a fresh new day.

She'd had her affair, confessed to it, and cried a gallon of tears, and her eyes were puffy, tender, and swollen; but she was happy and felt light and refreshed.

She tried not to disturb Walt as she eased out of bed, slipped on her white terrycloth bathrobe, and slid her feet into a pair of black leather slippers.

Tiptoeing out of the bedroom, she made her way to the hall and then downstairs to the kitchen. Her cell phone was in her purse, which was still in the car.

After she talked with Brenner and Irving, she'd call Myia Jordin and let her know she would not be in today.

Walt had already text Rhyan, informing her of his plans not to come in. He'd call his boss later today and let him know as well.

In fact, they intended to rearrange their work schedules to free themselves up for the next two weeks.

They knew it would take longer than that to mend their marriage, but right now, time together was a priority. They needed to stop the hemorrhaging of blood seeping from their marital bonds, threatening the wedding cord that had bound them together.

"We've got to press the pause button, figure out what went wrong, when it went wrong, and how to fix it," Walt had said last night.

She walked into the kitchen, which was bright and sunny as the natural light poured in through the windows. She couldn't help but smile at the cheerfulness of the room, such a contrast to the hell she'd gone through in this very room last night.

She'd make her call in the backyard on the outdoor seating area near the grove of pink crepe myrtles. But before heading out, she made herself a cup of tea.

As the kettle whistled, steam rose from the tiny spout. She turned off the stove, poured the hot water in her cup, and dropped in two sachets of white tea with rosebuds and jasmine. She stirred in a teaspoon of honey. She brought the cup to her nose and breathed in the tea's delicate bouquet, which she loved as much as the taste.

White tea with rosebuds and jasmine soothed her, and Helen knew she needed all the help she could get when making the call.

Chapter 63

CENTURIES AGO, THE POET RUMI WROTE,
"When love comes to kiss you, don't hold back."

That summed up her affair with Brenner and Irving. Surely, love
had come that day and kissed them, and neither Helen nor they had
held anything back.

After deactivating the alarm, she got her cell phone, made her way
back into the sunroom, opened and closed the sliding glass door, and
walked outside.

A chorus of tunes greeted her as singing and chirping wrens and
robins flitted through tree limbs with effortless ease.

Holding her teacup steady in her hand, she walked across the grass,
still damp with morning dew.

She wondered what she'd say to Brenner and Irving. How would
she start a conversation, knowing that by the end of it, they would no
longer be in her life?

She could still hear the cadence of their voices and laughter, but
mostly, she could still feel them moving inside her.

It took her just a few more steps to reach the large, covered patio at the far end of the in-ground pool. She sat on one of the dark wicker chairs with Sunbrella-covered cushions.

As she gazed at the nearby cluster of pink and white crepe myrtles, she lifted the cup to her mouth and blew a cooling breath before taking a generous sip of tea.

Leaning forward, she placed the cup on the wicker table, put the matching lid on top to keep the contents hot, sat back, and rested her head against the cushions.

With her legs crossed and her arms across her stomach, her eyes slid closed on their own volition.

She sat like that for a long, long moment, reliving that day at Heaven, The Restaurant. From the time she'd opened the door to the private dining room to the time they had said goodbye. Everything about that day was sweetly etched in her mind where it would stay for a lifetime.

She opened her eyes and sighed. A robin bravely landed on the arm of the wicker couch. "It's now or never," she said to the little bird as tears pooled in her eyes.

She reached inside the robe's pocket for her cell phone and dialed Brenner's number. When the phone rang, her heart skipped a beat.

But then she smiled and looked at the robin with its kind, beady eyes. "Brenner and Irving will be with me forever," she said to her patio companion, who looked at her as if he knew that, too.

Chapter 64

"HELLO, MY LOVE."

There was a deep richness in his voice that wrapped around her like a chocolate vine. She closed her eyes, feeling seduced by him all over again.

"Good morning, Brenner. I hope it's not too early to call." Just saying his name and hearing him sent a liquid chill through her body.

"You can call anytime. For you, no time is too early or too late," he said with a low rumble in his voice.

"I know how busy you both are, so I didn't want to disturb you." She tried to sound upbeat. "Where's Irving?"

"He's in the backyard with the photographer. They're figuring out places where we can stand to give us lots of different looks and backgrounds. But for you, we will stop whatever we're doing. You know that."

"You're such a sweet-talker."

"Are you okay, my love? I hear something in your voice."

She heard his concern.

"I'm okay."

"You sure? Why do I not believe you?"

"Brenner, I'm good." She paused and took a sip of tea. The robin, with its fat orange belly, looked at her with doubt in its eyes before flying off.

"I know you guys are getting excited." She leaned forward and put her teacup on the table.

"We are, and don't try to change the subject. I want to know what's wrong. Tell me."

She took a deep breath and let it out. *It's now or never.*

When she opened her mouth, her heartache was plain to hear.

"Brenner…umm, my…ah…my husband knows about the affair." Her voice wobbled as tears pooled in her eyes, but she quickly wiped them away.

"WHAT?! How did he find OUT?!"

She would never tell him about the calla lilies. It would hurt him and Irving too much. "Well… I told him."

"You did WHAT?!"

"I told him," she said with a little chuckle. "It's a long story."

"WOW! I'm speechless right now!"

"Well, I didn't tell him at first. Let's say it took a lively conversation before I did."

"Did he have proof or something?!"

She smiled, "Let's just say, counselor, he had his suspicions, and… umm, after a while, I stopped lying and finally told him the truth. He thinks I've only been with one man, and I…um, didn't correct that assumption."

"Suspicions? What kind of suspicions?"

She exhaled. "Umm, without going into a lot of details, let's just say he noticed a big change in me."

"Again, I'm speechless!" Brenner let out a loud sigh; he was simply flabbergasted.

"There's not much to say."

"He didn't hurt you, did he?" His genuine concern was apparent.

"No. No." Helen shook her head, "Nothing like that. Just hurt my feelings, that's all."

"Wow! Man!" His voice trailed off as he tried to wrap his head around this startling news. "So, how are you doing, really?"

"I'm good, and in a way, I'm a bit relieved."

"Let me guess. He told you to end the affair first thing this morning, didn't he?"

"He did."

"How do you feel about that?"

She did not respond at first. Instead, she breathed in and gazed at the grove of crepe myrtles, noticing how the sun kissed the tips of the blooms. She then gazed at their beautifully landscaped yard.

But after a moment, she shared her true feelings with Brenner. "I know this might sound strange, but I'm actually happy that he knows. I think this is a turning point in our relationship. One that we needed, quite frankly."

"I'll bet he's come to his senses and realizes what a true gift he has in you as his wife."

"Yes, I think so."

Brenner let out a breath. "You know I'm happy for you. I really am. Because you, my dear lady, deserve only the best."

"Thank you." She blotted the tears in her eyes with the robe's sash.

"Now, as for Irving and me, well, let me just say that we'll miss you. We were enjoying our conversations with you and looked forward to getting to know you more."

"I know," she said with a bit of regret in her voice. "I wanted that, too, and I was ready for Maui. Even though, truthfully, I had changed my mind about the trip. It wouldn't have been right."

"You're right. We had our moment, but I'll tell you this. He's one lucky man. I'll say that. And if polygamy was legal, we'd steal you away from your husband and make you ours."

She chuckled, beginning to feel lighter. "Umm, it sounds like you all are into women now!"

"I keep telling you, my love, we're only into you."

"Got it! Such a sweet- talker. By the way, I have a wedding gift coming to your house soon. It's supposed to arrive in early September. I'm just hoping it's not too big," she said, picturing the life-size work of art.

Noel had introduced her to the nationally acclaimed artist Ashya, who was known for vivid and colorful abstract portraits.

Helen had commissioned a forty-two-inch-by-seventy-five-inch piece of two men, one with a dark complexion and the other with a lighter complexion, in a loving embrace. She wanted the piece to be a bold statement for anyone who came into their home.

"You were our wedding gift," he said softly.

"I know." She smiled. "But I still wanted to get you guys something special."

"Whatever it is, we will adore it as we adore you."

He let out a long and melancholy sigh. "I love you, Helen, and just know that what we shared was beautiful."

Brenner's voice was stirring up all kinds of emotions as a rush of images and memories flooded her mind.

"Do you understand what I'm saying?"

"Yes, I do, but what we did was wrong," she whispered.

"My love, wrong and beautiful can co-exist. Remember that."

"I will, and you're right. While it was wrong, it was also too perfect and too wonderful."

"Irving and I will treasure our time with you until our dying days."

"Me, too." After a pause, she continued. "Speaking of Irving, I want to tell him myself."

"You know Irv's a diva and can be downright sensitive at times." Brenner laughed. "Let me break the news to him, and you can call him later today. Okay?"

"That will work."

"I'll probably have to give him mouth-to-mouth resuscitation, 'cause Miss Thang might pass out."

She laughed. "Well, give Irving the news gently and let him know that I'm definitely calling today."

"I will. Listen, if you need anything, and I don't care if you need to call at two in the morning, all you have to do is ask. Do you hear me?"

"My knight in shining armor," she whispered; she'd heard the love and sincerity in his voice.

"You know where we live and work, so even if you decide to delete our numbers from your cell, you'll always know how to contact us. And we'll know how to contact you."

"That's right. I know where to find you." There was sadness in her voice.

"Remember, you're a precious jewel, and wherever you go, I'm inside of you, and you're inside of me."

Tears pooled in her eyes, and in a brief silent moment, neither said a word as they clung to what they'd once had.

"I'm not go…going to say goodbye." Her voice wobbled. "I'm just going t…to say I love you both and wish you a life of love, health, and God's blessings."

"I won't say goodbye, either. I'll just wish you all the best that life has to offer."

"I love you, Brenner," she whispered. "I will never forget you or Irving."

"I love you, Helen."

She ended the call, placed the phone back in her pocket, and allowed her tears to run down her face.

She was ready to fall in love with Walt again, but for now, she would stay outside, sip her white tea with rosebuds and jasmine, and let her mind drift in whatever direction it wanted.

Epilogue

FOR THE PAST SEVEN MONTHS, HELEN and Walt had gone to one of the best marriage counselors money could buy.

Without fail, session after session, night after night, they laid out their marriage like a road atlas, retracing their steps back to the ditches, potholes, and wrong turns that had caused so much damage, wrecks, and collisions over the years.

At times, the counselor would sit back and give them a cup of ordinary hot black tea without sweetener. He called it "Tell It Now Truth Serum," and when they drank the tea, both had to tell the absolute truth with full transparency. No hiding even the tiniest detail.

It was during one of these sessions that Helen told Walt about the Ree & Mosley Agency, the ultra-exclusive restaurant where she'd met her date for dinner, and she confessed that she'd spent the day with not one man, but two.

She didn't divulge their names or the city they lived in, but she told him they were a gay couple and that one of the men had not been with a woman and wanted to do so before they married.

She told him they had sent her the bouquet of black calla lilies, and she shared with him that the flower had been the centerpiece on the table in the private dining room where she had spent hours with them.

Walt had termed her the "experimental pussy."

As Helen talked about her affair, it took every ounce of Walt's strength to listen, and while he did, tears rolled from his eyes; and sometimes, when he felt furious, there were no tears. That was when Walt would put on boxing gloves and repeatedly hit the cushiony six-foot-by-three-foot athletics wall pad the counselor had installed just for this purpose.

When it was his turn to talk, Walt made some confessions of his own.

He admitted to spending countless hours away from home while chasing the corporate dollar and neglecting to spend time with her instead of entertaining bank executives.

He confessed to losing sight of her as a sensual, alluring, and independent woman. Instead, he had grown too comfortable with seeing her as his dutiful wife and as a supportive mother to his son.

But after seven long months, they had done the painstaking and grueling work, and now they had the tools and bricks to build a bridge to their new relationship.

In two weeks, Walt would surprise Helen with a vacation to Jamaica; and this time, he would not invite bank executives. Only the sun, the sea breeze, and the yellow, white, and orange frangipani flowers were invited.

Lying in bed that evening with Walt's arms around her, tears pooled in Helen's eyes as she looked at the picture above the fireplace. It was of her on the aubergine- colored chaise lounge wearing the clingy white knit strapless dress.

He had replaced the painting that used to hang there.

Walt had contacted Leelynn Floyd and had her enlarge and frame this photo, which was his favorite, and he had also paid her to enlarge two other photos and send him another album with all of the boudoir photos Helen had taken that day. And yes, he had downloaded each photo of his wife on his cell phone.

But right now, as they lay in bed, Walt had a desperate need to dance with his honey.

Acknowledgements

WRITING THIS BOOK WAS A WONDERFUL, exhaustive and creative rush of excitement that would not have been possible without the loving support, encouragement and patience from my husband, and for that, I am incredibly grateful to him.

Also, a very warm thank you to my family and friends for their loving support; and a special thank you to my two girlfriends who suggested that I add questions at the end of the book.

A big sisterly hug to my sister for her unwavering support and love, who not only thoroughly read my book and gave excellent feedback, but who also took the time to write the "Some Thoughtful Questions" that are on the next page. Hopefully, these questions will stimulate further conversations about the story, the characters, particularly about Helen and Walt and Brenner and Irving.

A big, big thank you to my uncle, who again, took the time to carefully read my book and helped me identify any timeline issues, any misspelled words, and gave me a male perspective on how Walt mistook his role as a provider as his only role.

A book cover is the first impression a reader has of the book, and with a dynamic cover, hopefully the reader's attention is captured, and in that moment, they decide to open the book and dive right into the story. Well, I believe Barb Aronica did just that! In my opinion, she created a book cover that is not only dynamic but is simply captivating! Thank you, Barb! Also, thank you to the attorneys who provided outstanding legal support, and another big thank you to my editor, Jefferson, with First Editing for once again, providing excellent and timely service.

Lastly, in loving memoriam to my father and mother, and grandparents- for their unconditional love, nurturing and guidance.

Peace and blessings,

C.M. Harold

Some Thoughtful Questions!

1. How do you feel about Helen having an affair? Does it seem justified for her to have an affair with all that she has in her life: a beautiful home, a successful career, and a husband with a well- paying job?

2. Do you think Irving's desire to have sex with a woman (once) was an adulterous desire?

3. Why do you think Brenner and Irving sent Helen the bouquet of calla lilies?

4. How do you feel about Brenner's feelings for Helen? And after she begs to see him again, how do you feel about him asking her to join him and Irving on their honeymoon in Maui?

5. Do you think Helen should have confessed to having an affair? If so, should she have told Walt that she had been with two men? Do you think knowing that his wife had been with two gay men made Walt feel less troubled about her affair in any way?

6. When Helen calls Brenner to end the affair, do you feel that her crying is appropriate with her desires to stay with her husband? If you feel it is appropriate, then why? And if not, why not?

7. Do you think Walt completely forgives Helen for having an affair? Does she completely forgive him for his neglect over the years? Would you describe Walt's neglect as benign neglect?

8. Do you feel that dating services that have perfectly matched clients like Brenner and Helen often result in the individuals having sex on the first date?

9. If, given the opportunity to meet a good-looking man for lunch at an exclusive restaurant, who has been completely checked and cleared by a dating agency, would you go?

10. The elderly couple, Dr. Bill and Mrs. Macheria Bennett, make an appearance in book one and book two. What type of issues do you think they dealt with in the earlier years of their marriage that got them to the wonderful place they are now?

About the Author

C.M. HAROLD IS A NATIVE OF NORTH Carolina who now resides in Atlanta, Georgia. Her debut novel, *Dance with Honey: Unbought*, was published in March 2019. The sequel, *Dance with Honey: Determination and Forgiveness*, is the second novel in the Dance with Honey series.

While her books are fictional, modern-day romances, she hopes the stories inspire and motivate readers in real and meaningful ways to reignite the spark in their lives.

She is currently working on her next book titled, February Dame, an inspirational, nonfiction collection of essays of her conversations with extraordinary women. The book is named in honor of her mother, who was born in February, and through her loving, graceful and resilient manner, was a dame. Anticipate a release date of February 2023.

C.M. Harold enjoys talking about her writing and stories and would love to be a featured author at your next event. Please visit her website at dancewithhoney.com or follow her on Instagram at authorcmharold.

Thank you, and enjoy *Dance with Honey: Determination and Forgiveness*

CPSIA information can be obtained
at www.ICGtesting.com
Printed in the USA
LVHW101316060821
694699LV00006B/112/J